Mukai, Arise!

Itai Vhudzijena

Table of Contents

Synopsis

Drama.

Laugh Out Loud Humor!

Intrigue.

Adventure!

All this and more is what awaits you as you trace the pages of this book, 'Mukai, Arise!'

It is a true story of a dynamic, powerful, strong, courageous woman who hails from an African country situated in Southern Africa, known as Rhodesia, (present - day Zimbabwe)

The story traces the birth, life, struggles, challenges this girl/woman faced in a culture/society that not only did not protect children coming from single-parent households, but a society that also firmly believed that a woman's place is in the kitchen.

It's a story about survival, a commitment and dedication to succeed - a story about struggling, surviving and going on to thrive against ALL odds!

The legend of 'Mukai, Arise!' lives on.

Chapter 1 - The Beaming

'May God bless the woman deep within me, the woman I am trying to be.

May He mend where my heart is broken, and fill every empty space.

May God erase the fears of my past, to create in me a brighter future.

May He make me slow to anger and quick to forgive.

Amen'

"N'eeee!!'

A new born baby of royal blood gave her first cry on planet earth, signalling HER much awaited ARRIVAL!

The beaming from one planet to another was celebrated with an ear splitting wail, much to the joy and jubilation of the mother, the midwife and those waiting with baited breath outside by the door.

Usually when a baby cries, our instinct as a specie is to rush to it, take it in our arms, cuddle it and coo it so that it will either go back to sleep (if that's the intention) or to stop it from crying.

Yet, if its first entrance onto this planet is marked by silence, everyone in the room gets worried and panics.

The midwife or head nurse may even go to the extent of hitting the baby's bum in an effort to induce it to cry!!

That's how vital that first cry is; otherwise the baby runs the risk of not getting enough oxygen in its precious lungs in order to survive on planet earth.

A beautiful bouncy baby girl had just been delivered by its 16 year old mother.

A young girl herself. Barely a kid.

She had just delivered her first born, with big brown eyes, kinky hair, 3.3kg.

The instant the baby had come out, the midwife had placed the baby on its mother's belly and was now busy cutting the umbilical cord.

The mother had placed her right hand gently on her baby's shoulder, caressed it and whispered "Hallo there!!

Welcome to this world!!"

At the sound of its mother's voice, the baby opened its eyes and made its first eye contact with this vessel which had just teleported it into this universe.

The mother smiled and addressed the midwife

Mwanai?"

Her voice sounded hoarse with fatigue.

Beads of perspiration 'crowned' her forehead. A job well done indeed!!

"Musikana.

It's a baby girl."

The midwife replied still busying herself cleaning and tidying up the mother.

The new mother smiled and proceeded to count her baby's fingers and toes.

The first time she looked at them, she thought the baby had too many fingers and toes!

She had panicked and went onto count them one by one ... motsi ... piri ... tatu ...gumi!! ... one ... two ... three ... ten!!

She breathed a sigh of relief!

'Phew!'

Satisfied that her baby, indeed, had TEN fingers and TEN toes, the new mother sat back for a minute; resting.

It had been a long ordeal!

The mother had been in labour for more than 15 hours.

15 hours of contractions that came and went.

15 hours of confusion since being a new mother, she did not know what to expect. It was a new experience for her.

15 hours of the midwife poking and probing her body.

It had been such a huge relief when finally the midwife had asked her to push.

Felt really good !

The most interesting thing about childbirth is that one minute the mother is experiencing this enormous difficulty (labour); the next the baby is out; followed by intense relief.

The difficulty is forgotten the instant the baby pops out.

The mother, now very alert, focuses and concentrates on looking after her new born.

Its like the labour pains never happened!!

"Mwanai?!"

A male voice close by, outside by the door, could be heard enquiring about the gender of the child.

"Musikana!!"

The midwife announced joyfully and proudly

"Tell the king that he has a beautiful healthy baby girl!"

The Jinda raMambo sprinted at 160km/hr with the excellent news to his beloved king.

When he got to the royal court he knelt on the floor, placed his spear infront of him , took a bow in a gesture of reverence and respect and bellowed with pride "Ishe Mambo wangu - my King, I bring great tidings!!"

"Speak!"

Announced the King's Chief Advisor who was seated with him at the throne , to the right.

"Ishe Mambo wangu!

Shumba inoti ikadzvova musango, nyika yeeese inongendengeka; mhuka dzeeese dzoti mwakata mwakata kutiza! - my King, my hero, the bravest warrior known to man ... You have been blessed with a baby girl!!" He announced, beaming from ear to ear.

A bow tied to his back could be spotted.

He wore nhembe, a traditional type of clothing worn by the African Shona tribe in the early to mid 1900s.

The year was 1924.

"May the gods be praised!!"

The King announced joyfully lifting up his royal staff .

The whole royal court cheered.

Everyone broke into a lively banter, chattering with whoever was close by.

Lots of excitement was in the air.

Then one of the Senior royal court officials seated at the far corner facing the king asked joyfully "Ishe - my King, what will you call her?"

Without bating an eyelid, the king replied

"We shall call her, Mukai !"

"Hail to Princess Mukai!!"

Shouted the gentleman who had just asked the question

The royal court roared

"Hail to Princess Mukai!!"

The whole royal court gave three cheers headed by Jinda raMambo, the King's Head Warrior

"Hip, hip!!"

"Hooray!!"

"Hip, hip!"

"Hooray!!"

"Hip, hip!"

"Hooooraaaaay!!"

Resounded the whole royal court

Handikufara koko!!

Joyful ululation, beating of the drums and sounding of the trumpet and horns could be heard throughout the district!!

The king's youngest child had just been born to his younger wife, Matinetsa Kuzipachangwara !!

"Let the celebrations begin!!"

The king announced grinning from ear to ear.

He was a happy man; a proud father of many children.

At 75, he was still virile.

He had a 16 year old girl as his second wife to prove that point.

Back then, kings and chiefs married many wives.

The reasons for marrying so many wives varied from pure love to pure lust to purely for administrative purposes - strategic alliances.

Back then, the king could marry any woman he fancied, age difference be damned!!

Some kings were even notorious for having such a roving eye that they had a reputation for eyeing other men's beautiful wives and snatching them from under their noses. The husband of the fancied wife dared not protest if he valued his life.

He could be seen retreating away somewhere to lick his wounds like a wounded animal if such an unfortunate thing happened to him.

In some dunhu - districts, mothers used to hide their pretty young girl children from the king and his advisory council to shield and protect them from being 'snatched' by his roving eye and be added to the long list of 'the king's wives'.

In Matinetsa Kuzipachangwara's case, she had caught the king's roving eye one fateful day when she had gone kutsime - to the local well, to fetch some water for her mother's household needs.

King Mukundu Chapfumbu happened to be passing by the same route with his royal entourage. He was travelling in the opposite direction going back to his royal palace, when their paths crossed.

It is said that the minute he laid eyes on her akadengezera hari yakazara mvura, carrying a clay pot full of water ontop of her head, something had stirred in him.

Was it love or was it lust?

What he knew for sure was that his heart had stopped beating for a 'full minute'!!

Never in his life had he beholden such a beautiful sight.

It is said he had ordered his entourage to stop and had jumped off his carriage.

Word has it that he had marched towards Matinetsa.

He had stopped her in her tracks and asked for some water to drink.

Matinetsa had sat her clay pot down on the ground, taken a mukombe - gourd, took some water from her clay pot and politely handed it to the King.

The king had accepted the water and drank it.

It is said the king had confided to his closest counsel later that, that had been the coolest, tastiest water he had ever tasted in his 70+ years.

And he had been smitten too!

Enchanted and mesmerized by her beauty, King Mukundu Chapfumbu is said to have pursued Matinetsa with the zest and strength of a 40 year old!

He wanted her to be his second wife.

The man who had managed to live and be contented with only one woman, the Queen, for all these years, was now considering taking on a second wife!!

Shocking!!

Baffling!!

Surely he was way past mid-life crisis?!

At 74, he was 34 years too late!!

Usually mid-life crisis happened to both men and women from about 40!!

The Queen could not understand it when he informed her of his intention to marry a second wife.

"But she is old enough to be your granddaughter?!!"

His wife, the Queen had protested in the privacy of their chambers.

"Why don't you let one of your children marry her?

Amon is still single.

He can be persuaded to take her on as his wife!" The Queen had tried to make him see sense.

"No!

My mind is made up, woman!! I want her as MY wife!

Amon can find his own!"

The king had bellowed

"But ...!"

The Queen had tried to protest

"No, buts!

If you don't like my decision, you can pack your bags and go back to your parents' home.

But the girl is coming!

And she will be coming as my second wife!

You will treat her with respect!

Is that clear?!"

The king had been furious

The Queen remained silent.

True to her independent nature, Matinetsa had initially refused the king's offer of his hand in marriage.

Reason?!

Isn't it obvious??!!

He was too old!!

For crying out loud, the man was old enough to be her grandfather!!

She was about 60 years his junior !!

Matinetsa was described as this phenomenally beautiful girl, with a vivacious and outgoing personality.

Her character and manner was totally unlike all the girls of her time.

Her fierce independent nature was revered by some and hated by others.

King Mukundu Chapfumbu fell in the former category.

Finally after three attempts, Matinetsa had accepted the king's hand in marriage.

Reason?!

Partly due to fear that if she really refused his hand in marriage outright, something 'bad' would happen to her and her beloved mother and partly because the lure of being the King 's younger wife - vaNyachide - came with its packs ...

Love and commitment to the relationship was definitely NOT in the picture.

Matinetsa came from the Gutu District in Masvingo Province.

Masvingo Province is located in the southeastern part of Zimbabwe.

It has a population of 1.485 million as of the 2012 census, ranking fifth out of Zimbabwe's ten provinces.

Established as Victoria Province by the British South Africa Company, it was one of the five original provinces of Southern Rhodesia.

In 1982, two years after Zimbabwe's independence, it was renamed Masvingo Province.

The province is divided into seven districts, including Masvingo District, which contains the provincial capital Masvingo City.

Established in the late 19th Century, Gutu is the third largest district in Masvingo Province after Chiredzi and Mwenezi.

With a population of 203,083 it is the northern most District in the province.

It is divided into Gutu West, Gutu North, Gutu Central, Gutu South and Gutu East.

The name 'Gutu' is historically reported to have emerged from 'Chinomukutu wemiseve' meaning, 'the one with a load of arrows'

This is according to oral historical folklore of the 'Gumbo' clan who are said to have taken over the area from the 'Shiri' clan through killing them by poisoning their fruit trees in the 'Gona' area.

Mupandawana is the largest district service centre.

It was designated as a 'growth point' during the early years of independent Zimbabwe together with such places as Gokwe in the Midlands Province and Juru in Mashonaland East province. Mpandawana gained town status in April 2014.

The population is mostly the Karanga, a Shona sub-tribe.

Gutu Rural District Council is in charge of the day-to-day running of the district.

The birth of Mukai in the month of May 1924 was celebrated far and wide.

People drank, people sang, people danced.

The King was overjoyed!!

Six months later, the cloud turned ...

King Mukundu Chapfumbu suddenly took ill and died a week later ....

After reigning his district for more than 56 years, King Mukundu Chapfumbu breathed his last.

Mukai, Arise!

Chapter 2 - What Now?

'If their name isn't God, then their opinion doesn't matter and their approval isn't needed' ~curiano.com

"The King is dead!!"

Word spread in the entire kingdom.

Yoooweee!!!

There was mheremhere nemhirizhonga mudunhu rese - loud cries, chaos and confusion everywhere !!

'What are we going to do?'

'Who will succeed him?'

Lamentations could be heard echoing across the whole district!

Those who had loved and respected him, wailed, wept and sobbed; beating their fists against their chests and throwing themselves to the ground.

Those who did not care much for him, did not. They just stared blankly infront of them.

Matinetsa fell in the category of those who 'did not'.

She had been still trying to get used to the idea that she was now a married woman.

Now barely 15 months later, she had to get used to this new idea that she had recently been widowed!

And worse, she had a six month old baby on her hands to take care of!!

Ah!

What a lot to take on for such a young woman.

What was she going to do now?

She hadn't stayed long enough at the royal palace to bond with the king's first wife, the Queen.

Barika rakaoma!

Being the younger wife, she got the lion's share of their communal husband's love, attention, affection and TIME.

As a result, the first wife, the Queen, was naturally jealousy of her.

She and her seven children, resented, disliked and scoffed at her.

In the previous 15 months, life at the royal palace had not been easy for Matinetsa.

The constant stares, the hostility in the air, the constant bickering was more than Matinetsa could bare.

Even though Matinetsa had her own hut and tried to keep to herself as much as possible, the Queen and her children, particularly the one called Amon, was very nasty and cruel to her.

Amon and Matinetsa were of the same age group and he felt that Matinetsa was a gold digger who had married his father, the King, for his fame and wealth.

Amon's dislike and resentment of her ran deep.

In fact, his hostility towards her made Matinetsa fear for her life.

She was so afraid and so suspicious of Amon that she never left her hut unlocked, just in case Amon poisoned her food.

She carried her baby everywhere.

You see, human beings are not like wild animals.

We do not mind sharing such things as food, our home, ideas ... even our personal space.

But when it comes to the person we are either dating or married to; we do not like to share.

Sharing always leads to disaster.

It is never a wise thing to marry more than one wife or more than one husband.

Petty jealousies get in the way.

Competition for affection becomes the order of the day.

The funeral of the king lasted a month.

Mourners came far and wide.

Fellow kings, queens, princes, princesses, chiefs, tribesmen from other districts came to pay their last respects.

King Mukundu Chapfumbu was known throughout the region.

He was of the Shumba totem - the lion tribe.

He was revered and feared by many, for not only did he have a reputation for being a wise and fair leader, he was also famous for being The Commander - In - Chief of one of the most powerful armies in the region.

He could easily have quashed smaller and weaker tribes around his district, but he chose to live in harmony with them; allowing them to have their own chiefs and pay homage to their own Mwari - God.

As was customary at the time, when a king died, his wife and children along with his assets were divided or apportioned equitably between his brothers and nephews.

The shocking thing is that, even if the brother or nephew was already married, he was free to take on another wife from this entourage, if he so desired.

The ages of the brothers and nephews ranged from 18 to 80.

In Shona traditional culture, this is referred to as kugara nhaka.

What happens is that on this day, the king's wives would sit in a straight line in order of seniority.

The first wife, referred to as The Queen, would be first in the line up; followed by the second wife and so forth.

The second wife et al were referred to as Princesses.

There was only one Queen.

This title was reserved for only the first wife; who also had the privilege of bearing him sons who succeeded him in his throne.

All the other kids who were subsequently born by the next string of wives took the title of prince and princess, depending on the gender.

Once the wives lined up in order of seniority, the presiding Officer would announce, "Who here takes the first wife?!"

The concerned man would stand, carry a dish full of water to the first wife, place it by her feet.

If she washed her hands, that was taken as a sign that she accepted him.

The same process was repeated for the second and subsequent wives until all of them had been accounted for.

It was understood that the man was accepting both the woman plus her children.

From that moment on, she packed her belongings and moved to his home. She became his full responsibility.

When King Mukundu Chapfumbu died, due to old age, all his assets, wives and children included were supposed to be equitably distributed.

This event was quite a big thing in the entire district.

It was like a public auction.

A year after the funeral, a special day was set up when the apportionment would take place.

And mind you, during that entire year, the brothers and nephews of the king were free to liaise, solicit, approach any of the wives that they fancied and ask for their hand in marriage.

If she said 'yes', then on that agreed date, the concerned brother or nephew would 'stake his claim' - the wife PLUS her children.

In the subsequent year that followed, after the death of King Mukundu Chapfumbu, all roads led to Matinetsa Kuzipachangwara's household!

Droves upon droves of suitors could be seen flocking and lining up, trying their luck at pleasing the young and eligible, now 'bachelorette', Matinetsa.

Men of all ages ... 18 ... 20 ... 30 ... 40 ... 50 ... 70 ... even 90 ... could be seen popping in and out of Matinetsa's compound, volunteering this ; volunteering that in an attempt at being 'helpful'.

The helpful household chores ranged from offering to chop wood and stake it up for her by the back of her hut ... carry heavy objects for her ... go hunting and bring freshly caught kudu for her ... go fishing and bring freshly caught large bream or some other type of fish.

Those menfolk whose natural talent was catching wild birds, such as njiva - doves ; hanga Guinea fowl; etc, eagerly set out in the forest to catch their prey and brought it to her without being asked.

Road runners became her staple diet!!

Those who were good in gathering wild fruit, such as matamba, mazhumwi, man'ono, shumha, chakata, nzvirumombe, tsambatsi etc carried and brought them to her.

Ko kuzoti majuru !! ...

Waiwana murume mukuru akagara pachuru achijuruja majuru ... ko iko kurumwa nawo?!!

Aa , haiwa!!

Waingonzwa 'yuwi !' 'yuwi!' kuri kuyuwira murume mukuru!! Ko kuenda kumba!!

Aa ... imi!!

Ko idzo ishwa ... ?!!

Gore iroro, dzakabuda dzakawanda zvakatokatyamadza munhu wese maGutu, kwaMataruse!!

Ko makurwe ... kuita shara ude chaiko!

Translation!

Matinetsa was also treated to local delicacies that were very popular at the time since they were a source of rich protein.

Her household became very affluent.

If she was business minded, she could have sold most of these 'gifts' and would have made a killing in the process!!ʙ

Matinetsa may have been young, but she was not naive.

She was very aware that each of the men who brought any of these provisions to her house was not doing so out of the kindness and goodness of their hearts to help out a widow.

She was fully aware that each one of them had an ulterior motive.

She chuckled to herself.

Hanzi 'zino rinonyemwerera warisingadi'

In an attempt at courtesy and trying to be neighbourly, Matinetsa found herself smiling even at those people she could not stand.

She found herself saying such things as

'Thank you!'

'Oh, you shouldn't have!!'

'That was very thoughtful of you!'

'Wow!

What have I done to deserve so much meat?!' 'To what do I owe the pleasure of your company?!'

The list went on and on.

Meanwhile, all these activities did not go unnoticed by the queen who hardly had any suitors stepping infront of her door.

All possible suitors' eyes were fixed firmly towards Matinetsa's household.

If there was any chance that the Queen and Princess Matinetsa would be drawn closer as a result of their shared common loss; the King, these events certainly saw to it that the wedge between them became even wider.

To say the Queen 's jealousy index climbed up a notch higher, is an understatement that spanned generations!

She was livid!

She was furious!

She was beyond angry!

'Who the hell did this girl think she was?!

Attracting all these men with her coy, gay laughter!!'

Life was not fair!

SHE, as the Queen, was supposed to be the ONE getting all this attention!!

Not that girl!

First, she had snatched her husband away from her!

Now, she was 'snatching' all these potential suitors from her!!

Life was not fair indeed!!

She fumed

On the other hand, Matinetsa watched all this activity and hullabaloo with a sense of alienated majesty, chuckling to herself.

If only they all knew!!

So on the designated day, all people; near and far ; short and tall; slim and not so slim; men, women, children ... made their way to the royal court.

Too bad there were no mobile phones back then; otherwise, we would have seen lots of selfies being posted on Facebook, Twitter and Instagram covering this event!!

One of the king's eldest brothers was the one presiding over the event.

First on the agenda was the apportionment of his assets.

Things went smoothly in this category.

It was a straight forward procedure since official documents existed that stretched a long span of years stating what exactly he owned and who was entitled to what.

So, Assets equitably distributed ... check!

Second on the agenda was the kugarwa nhaka procedure.

When it came to wives and children distribution, the Queen was the first in the line up.

The presiding Officer said

"Who here Volunteers kugara nhaka, the Queen?!"

This question was followed by absolute silence.

No one moved.

No one spoke.

No one looked up.

Apparently there were no suitors who came forward to propose to take over her and her affairs.

Infuriated, the Queen had glared at every man around the royal court.

They all averted their eyes for fear of being pinned down, and be forced to be the next husband.

The presiding Officer then said "Alright!

We move on!"

Looking around he asked

"Is Princess Matinetsa Kuzipachangwara present here at this court ?!"

Everyone looked around; then a lone figure that had been sitting a distance away from everyone else clutching a baby, stood up and walked towards the front to face the dare - royal court.

All eyes were focused on this lone figure.

As she stood facing the royal court , everyone recognized Princess Matinetsa with her six month old baby.

She was holding her baby in her arms.

"I am here, sir!"

Matinetsa addressed the royal court.

"Princess Matinetsa, you are next.

Tell us, of all the king's brothers and nephews here-present, which one do you choose to be your next husband?!"

The presiding officer asked

All eyes were on Matinetsa.

They waited with baited breath.

Matinetsa looked at the precious jewel in her hands and said "Neither!"

"What?!"

The presiding officer had not understood

"I don't choose any man!" Matinetsa shouted

A hush silence followed

No one in the crowd spoke.

No one in the royal court dared breathe.

What had just transpired?

The presiding officer looked at his counsel who starred back at him with stony faces.

This was a big embarrassment to all the menfolk in the king's lineage.

By this statement, Matinetsa was alluding to the suggestion that no man in the king's lineage was worthy to be her next husband.

But according to the law yekugarwa nhaka, if either the man or woman concerned did not want kugarwa nhaka, then he or she was well within his or her rights to do so. No one forced either party.

With this in mind, the presiding Officer took a deep breath and said "Fair enough.

Dare rino - this court has heard what you have just said, Princess Matinetsa.

So, what do you prefer to do?

Continue living here in your house at the royal palace, or go back to your parents home?"

Matinetsa did not even bat an eye lid.

She said

"I prefer to go back to my parents' place. I will take Princess Mukai with me."

There was a hush silence.

Everyone was stunned at this turn of events!!

This was indeed, unprecedented!

Never in their district had they ever heard a woman assert herself in this way and so young too!

"Very well.

You can go ahead and return to your parents' home.

You can take your baby with you."

The presiding Officer acquiesced

Matinetsa said "Thank you"

And with that, it was bye bye King Mukundu Chapfumbu's royal palace and its chinanigings.

Princess Matinetsa Kuzipachangwara sang a favourite tune of hers all the way to her hut, packed all her belongings, carried her baby girl on her back - kubereka kumusana - looked around her home one last time, smiled, silently bade it goodbye and off she went, back to her parents ' home!

Back to a place of safety, tranquility, full of acceptance and decency.

A chapter had just ended.

Another one lay ahead of her ... stretched out ... waiting ... beckoning ..., with its doors wide open ... winding and turning, meandering like an ox bow lake along the Zambezi ...

Mukai, Arise!

Chapter 3 - Full Circle

The enemy always fights the hardest when he knows God has something great in store for you.

"You are back?!"

Matinetsa 's mother asked

She too had been widowed these past 10 years.

So she had an inkling as to what her daughter was actually going through right at this time.

Vakudandaya, Matinetsa's mother, was described as a very loving, gentle and caring woman.

Whereas her daughter, Matinetsa, was described as 'fiesty', stubborn and single-minded to the point of qualifying as selfish; Vakudandaya was the exact opposite.

She was described as sober minded, fair, hard working.

Her gentle character and love for family was one of her hallmarks.

Her patience was described as not knowing any bounds.

Widowed with four children - two sons, Vangana and Tsikai plus two daughters, Matinetsa Kuzipachangwara and Njiva - the four were said to be the apple of their mother's eye.

Spoilt to the core, Matinetsa knew that the world revolved only around her.

When Matinetsa returned to her mother's house, she quickly relegated all her motherly duties to her mother; who gladly took up her upkeep of her granddaughter, Mukai, with a gentle and loving heart.

Whilst her mother was busy looking after Mukai, Matinetsa was now as free as a bird, single again, back in the 'scene' ... the dating scene!

Now, 17 years old and looking as ravishing as ever, it wasn't long before suitors were lining up at The Kudandaya homestead, hoping and praying that they would be the ones chosen to be the next Matinetsa Kuzipachangwara's husband!!

Oh, Matinetsa had charm alright!!

She knew how to weave any man's heart on her little finger!!

She had the style; the grace; the personality; the know-how.

Hardly a year later, Matinetsa accepted a hand in marriage to a man who lived a few kilometres away from her home.

The lucky gentleman's name was Mavhoro.

Mukai was 15 months old.

Matinetsa left her baby daughter with her mother and went onto start a new life with her new husband.

Fortunately for Mukai, her grandmother, Vakudandaya, took great care of her such that she did not miss her own mother.

I guess one could say that Vakudandaya became the surrogate mother Mukai needed.

Yes, Vakudandaya was THAT loving!!r

Hats off to all mothers who have such a capacity to love.

The world is that much better because of such precious additions in society.

The irony of Mukai's story is that, much as her grandmother filled in the shoes of being a loving and present parent, Vakudandaya could not protect her from the sentiment and bullying society can throw at a child whose parents are not present to protect her or him.

When Matinetsa left to start her new life, she hardly visited her baby.

Gossip mongers and those who simply are mean by nature started spreading rumours around the Gutu district.

'Mukai - the orphan ...!'

'Mukai - the child without parents ... !'

'Fushai ... oops!! I meant Mukai!!'

On and on the insults continued.

Mukai being a fighter by nature, would retaliate against these bullying tactics by engaging in fist fights - literally!!

Mukai was described as a girl who did not take crap from anyone. She spoke her mind; self control and mastery be damned!!

There is a saying,

'What you focus on expands'

This is so true.

For, the more Mukai focused on what her peers said ... jeering ... taunting her ... traumatizing her ...

... the more those jeers and tauntings multiplied.

They were like rabid dogs ... all over her!

Bullying ... emotional abuse ... physical abuse ... became young Mukai 's breakfast, lunch and dinner!

It became her daily bread.

As a result, Mukai found it difficult to make friends.

Making friends requires bonding ... how could she when in her own infancy, she had never bonded with her own mother, let alone, her father!!

First, her father had been snatched away from her by the cruelest abandoner known to mankind, DEATH!!

As if that was not enough, the second wave of abandonment had made its presence known when her mother had left her to marry another man.

Even though she was fond of her grandmother and grateful for her maternal care, still there was a part of her that missed her mother.

Matinetsa never visited her daughter, so in the little girl 's mind, that too, qualified as abandonment.

The third wave of abandonment came when society rejected her by calling her all sorts of names.

Society can be cruel at times.

Gutu people of that time, were no exception!! KwaMataruse!!

When a child loses its parents, it no longer has that cushion; that protection from society 's sick and twisted belief systems.

Orphans of that genre can testify to this fact.

Even though, in truth, strictly speaking, Mukai was not an orphan because she had a living parent, her Mum; those who bullied her did not care for actual facts.

As long as bending the truth a little made for a joke or two - a few laughs, at the expense of the chosen 'candidate', then by all means it served as great entertainment and amusement for the day.

And when you think about it, what is wrong with being an orphan?

What does it matter whether a child has living parents or doesn't?

Don't we have a fiduciary duty as society to PROTECT orphans?

Then how come we allow such abominations to take place where some children from wayward families are allowed to get away with making these children's lives a living hell?

I pose that question to the Gutu people of that time, who allowed such things to happen.

I also pose this question to anywhere else across the globe where such bullying tactics are still allowed to flourish unchecked.

Thankfully, Mukai was a fighter and did not allow these bullying tactics to get her down.

Instead, she used these humiliating practices as impetus to propel her forward.

After all there is a saying,

'When things get tough, you must get tougher!' ~Bob Proctor

Mukai was a staunch believer and advocate of this line of thinking.

Whilst her school mates sat up in trees and threw stones at teachers, Mukai buried her nose in her books.

Whilst girls of her age group mixed and mingled with potential suitors, Mukai recited her mental arithmetic.

Whilst her perpetrators spent sleepless nights brainstorming on ways of how to make her life more miserable, Mukai spent sleepless nights brainstorming on which College she was going to enrol into next after graduating from Secondary school.

As a result, it wasn't long before Mukai started excelling in school.

She was top of her class from Primary School right through Secondary school.

Noticing how brilliant she was, The Dutch Reformed Church adopted her.

The generous and wonderful woman who adopted Mukai was called Miss Principle.

Miss Principle paid for her school fees in return for her doing odd jobs at the church.

This scenario suited her perfectly and continued right up until she graduated with honours in secondary school.

1937 - the year Mukai Mukundu Chapfumbu passed with a First Class in Standard Six.

Yes, ladies and gentlemen, Mukai studied all the way to Standard Six and went onto College to specialize as a Primary School Teacher.

She enrolled at Morgenster Teacher's College - an institution of The Reformed Church in Rhodesia.

True to being the 'Light of The Nation' - Matthew 5 vs 14, after graduation, in 1941, Mukai got a job at Maregedze Primary School in Gutu, in the then, Rhodesia.

She taught Grade 3 and received a salary every month.

Mukai was now a woman of independent means!!

10 : 0 !!

Those boys and girls who used to make fun of her and taunt her were now left miles behind ... still in the jungles and trees that they belonged, ape-like.

They had not even finished Grade 2!!

Now all they could do was kupunyaira neshungu!!

Some even had the nerve to approach her and ask for a cash advance!!

They say

'The best revenge is success'

They are right!!

Mukai Mukundu Chapfumbu got her own back by being phenomenally successful.

But life was not done with her yet.

There was still a lot coming her way ... ox bow lake - like, her life kept meandering ...

Mukai, Arise!

Chapter 4 - Realignment 101

There is a saying

'Lightning never strikes twice!' to mean that someone who has been very lucky or unlucky is unlikely to have the same good or bad luck again.

They are wrong!!

In Mukai's case, it did!!

Life threw her a curve ball when one fateful day, she met and fell head over heels in love with a certain eligible bachelor who had attended the same College as her!!

Now, they taught at the same school.

This handsome young bachelor, sharp as a whistle, had also completed Standard Six and gone onto specialise as a Primary School teacher at Morgenster Teachers' College.

The handsome bachelor also came from the same area of Gutu district.

His mother was also the younger wife of a local king.

Unlike Mukai, this handsome fellow came from a very loving and close-knit family.

His father, the king, only had two wives ... the first wife, the Queen and the second wife, his mother.

What happened was that, unlike the Queen, Mutereri's mother by the name of VaZvirehwa Mutepfe - nicknamed VaChihera with a baptismal name of Elizabeth, had been blessed with two children, a son by the name of Mutereri and a daughter by the name of Chandirekera.

This was not because VaChihera could not conceive children!

Oh she conceived alright!!

And on a regular basis throughout her marriage to the king.

The challenge she faced was that she used to conceive NOT one, but TWO babies at a time!!

Yes, she used to conceive twins.

The unfortunate thing that used to happen was that, during this time, in the early to mid 1900s; it was Shona custom to kill one twin.

It was like culling the 'herd'.

The accepted practice was that when both babies were born, the midwife would select one, usually the frail one and go away and kill it, leaving the mother with one baby.

This practice was done in the interest of saving 'BOTH' babies.

They had to be cruel to be kind, I guess.

They felt that bearing in mind the meagre resources, the mother struggled to nurse and look after just one baby, let alone, two!

So, in order to at least give a chance to the stronger baby, they killed the weaker one.

Unfortunately, for VaChihera, she used to give birth to identical twins.

Whenever the mid-wife culled the weaker twin, it wasn't long before the surviving twin would become ill and die shortly thereafter.

This was the drill and pattern for several years in VaChihera's marital life.

Those days graves were in the compound, so it is said that she was surrounded by her six children's graves - the other twins could not even be acknowledged.

By the time she finally conceived ONE baby in her seventh pregnancy, she had, all but lost hope of ever holding a baby in her arms who would live past the age of two!!

So, when this baby boy arrived on this planet, ALONE, VaChihera was over joyed!!

She thanked her living God for this precious gift and promised that she would treasure this gift always.

Because of the nature of the string of deaths that had preceded the arrival of this beautiful bouncy baby boy, 3.1kg in weight; VaChihera named the boy, Mutereri.

So, in the month of August 1921, Mutereri was born to the younger wife of King Mutubuki, son and heir to King Zimunya.

Soon after that, VaChihera conceived a second baby, who was also not a twin.

She named this baby girl, Chandirekera, meaning 'whatever it is that is causing me all this misfortune (of having a string of babies who die or are killed in their infancy), may it have mercy on me.

Dai chandiregererawo!

May it forgive me!'

Mutereri was treated to lots of love and affection, not only from his father, the King; but from his four beloved and besotted girl cousins, Fungai, Gamuchirai, Upenyu and Ndakarwirwa.

These four sisters had been born to a father by the name of Rapingwa, and going by a Christian name of Amon.

Their mother was called Svongwei.

Mutereri was the boy the king had agonized over for years.

Finally he had been blessed with one!

God was great indeed!!

Hence, Mutereri was treated like a prince - which he was anyway, since he was the son of a king and heir to his father's kingdom.

He was also treated like a prince by his mother, VaChihera, who in her heart, he was the child who was a long time coming.

In short, Mutereri was born with a 'silver spoon' in his mouth, literally.

During his infancy, the mother is said to have kept a dish full of water by her hut.

If anyone happened to pass by her house and wanted to come inside to see and touch her baby, they had to FIRST WASH THEIR HANDS!!

Mutereri grew up with everything he wanted.

He only had to say it, and it materialized.

Life was definitely his oyster!!

As a result, he was spoilt rotten.

He never had had to work for anything in his life!

Everything came easy for Mutereri.

If it was food he needed, his mother was at his back and call.

If it was good grades he needed at school, he had the brains for it.

If he needed anyone to defend him against bullies at school or in society at large, his four girl cousins fought his battles for him.

They were there to throw the punches, literally!!

King Mutubuki was of the Soko Vhudzijena tribe. His father before him, the one he succeeded, was King Zimunya who also had a brother called Musabayana.

King Zimunya's father had been King Nematumbai Barwanowako.

They were part of the Bantu tribe that had originally migrated from East Africa, past Kenya, initially settling in Wedza and had now been co-existing with King Mukundu Chapfumbu, who was of the Shumba tribe in the Gutu district.

They say 'opposites attract'.

In Mukai and Mutereri 's case, even though these two came from very different backgrounds and experiences, the two became fast friends.

Mukai was from The Shumba totem, whilst Mutereri was from The Soko Vhudzijena totem.

They spent every free time together, talking, chatting, brainstorming.

When they were together, they were in their own world! No one else existed.

They could spend hours together.

With time, their friendship developed into something much more meaningful ... deeper. They fell in love

Within a year, Mukai and Mutereri were married.

Now at 22 years of age, it is said that Mukai was the happiest she had ever been in her entire life!

She thought that finally, she had gotten a break in life.

Now she could have a family of her own ... a loving and caring husband ... children ... and live a healthy, happy life.

As was custom at the time, when a woman got married, she left her parents' home and transferred to go live with her new husband's family.

She was not allotted a house of her own to live in with her new husband, but was expected to live in the same house with her in-laws.

Now, such a set up works best if the in-laws like and get along well with each other.

What happens in a situation where the in-laws are fighting tooth and nail for their brother/ cousin NOT to associate, let alone, MARRY, a woman of his choice?

What happens in a situation where the daughter-in-law who is coming to join this family is an independent, strong, powerful woman who is used to fighting her own battles and winning? 'Killing her own spiders!' as they say.

What happens in a situation where the man one has married, never had to fight for anything or anyone in his entire life before?

This is the fate that befell Mukai Mukundu Chapfumbu.

After she got married to Mutereri, as expected, she moved in with her in-laws.

These included Mutereri's four possessive girl cousins who felt that:

1. Their cousin brother could do no wrong They worshipped the ground he walked on.

2. No one was good enough for their cousin brother; and that, unfortunately, included Mukai

3. Their cousin brother 's choice of wife was wrong.

It was a combination of all these three misconceptions that orchestrated the tug of war between Mukai, on one hand; and her cousin sisters-in-law, on the other; with Mutereri stuck firmly right in the middle!

It was a combination of all these three misconceptions that caused the most heartache and fights in the Mutereri household.

It was a combination of all these three misconceptions that created a massive rift between Mukai and Mutereri, so early on in their marriage ... a rift that was as vast, deep and wide as the The Great Rift Valley of Kenya.

In theory, theirs should have been a marriage made in heaven, what with the two of them being fellow professionals ... they were both teachers, hence, originated from the same planet!

Secondly, before marriage, they had been the best of friends; told each other everything; spend a lot of time together; did everything together.

So, what changed?

The four cousin sisters-in-law are said to have ganged up, wolf-like, howling and screaming at their cousin brother's wife like there was no tomorrow.

Nothing she ever did in that household was ever good enough.

They found fault with, literally, everything she did.

There was not enough salt in the beef stew.

The cooking pot was not cleaned properly.

The water she fetched from the local well was not enough for the entire household

You spend too much time at that school of yours; now you say you have marking of Test Scripts?!!

The accusations stretched a mile

The shouts and screams were reported to be so loud and vicious that it is said neighbours, near and far, used to come and listen.

What a spectacle!

The sad and tragic thing about Mukai's demise at this stage, was that once again, she found herself at the centre of bullying, this time from the people she trusted the most, the people she called family, the people she lived with under the same roof; her own cousin sisters-in-law !!

Yes, ladies and gentlemen, lightning DOES strike twice!

The four sisters were of the opinion that:

1. They didn't like Mukai's family background.

They felt she came from a broken home with a surviving parent who was never around.

Hence, in their opinion, she in turn, would not make a good mother and wife to their cousin brother.

2. They felt she was 'too educated', hence, was too independent.

They were from the 'old school' that was of the mistaken impression and belief that mukadzi akadzidza anonetsa!! - an educated woman is a trouble maker in the home.

They felt that by her being of independent means and having a career of her own, meant she had an opinion on what was to transpire in the home.

That, they did not like !!

And imagine, such sentiments were coming from fellow women!!

Shocking!!

Another sad and tragic fact is that, if you look closely into relationships in the families, a fellow woman suffers the most under the mischievous and petty jealousies of a fellow WOMAN in the family - not a man !!

The actual person behind the scenes who would be orchestrating the disharmony and 'quietly encouraging' or inciting the bad behaviour of the man, may be:

a jealous and possessive mother-in-law. a jealous and possessive sister-in-law.

a jealous and manipulative friend.

It may even be a jealous sister or step-sister.

It's sad, but true.

In Mukai Mukundu Chapfumbu's case, instead of the four cousins to hold fort and unite with their new sister-in-law, and fight the battle of life as a single unit, they allowed such base things as petty jealousies and terrible misconceptions dictate how they regarded, felt and behaved towards their otherwise, extremely generous, hard working, loving, diligent, conscientious and results-oriented daughter-in-law.

Fortune had, indeed, favoured them greatly by placing such a daughter-in-law on their laps, yet they were so emotionally poverty stricken, they mistook the wood for the trees.

They failed to recognize the jewel that had just landed on their laps!

Fortune had indeed, favoured Mutereri, but he was too full of himself to truly realise the gift that he had just been given - the gift of a steady, straight forward, loving spouse who was committed to him and his family.

Hapana nhamo inodarika iyoyo!

Poverty of the soul!

All Mutereri needed to do, was to be a man for once, offer his wife his backbone; be there for her, create a solid and firm alliance with his wife and not allow third parties to get between them and destroy their happy home.

It is clear, for a marriage to hold firm, the two people in the relationship must put each other first, before anyone else.

They must be united in thought and in deed.

They must work as a single unit and not allow outside sentiments to rule their home.

In truth, noone has a right to come between a man and a woman who are married and try to force his or her opinion on them.

Anyone who listens and goes on to execute whatever the perpetrator is suggesting is nothing but a fool, for sooner or later, that relationship will suffer with detrimental consequences.

In this case, guess who suffered the most in this tug of war which went on unchecked?!

Mutereri!!

He found himself caught up in the middle!

And both camps wanted him to choose a side!

What happened is that, whenever his wife fought in a war of words with his cousin sisters whilst he was out, when he came back, he was confronted by a very angry wife who would repeat everything that had transpired in his absence.

The intention of reporting all this to him was so that he could do something about it.

Conversely, the four cousin sisters would take him to task about what his wife had said to them in his absence.

In a similar vein, the reason for this reporting was so that Mutereri would do something about his wife.

Unfortunately, Mutereri loved BOTH his wife and his four cousin sisters and would not take sides.

BIG MISTAKE!!

As a result, his wife felt that he was 'weak' as a man, for he could not come to the defense of his wife.

She felt that by him choosing NOT to confront his cousin sisters and calling them to order, he in effect, was in agreement with their sentiment.

This was a bitter pill to swallow for both of them.

Conversely, the sisters felt that he was 'weak' as a man, for he would not side with them, divorce this wrong choice of wife, and marry someone else who fit their idea and description of what constitutes the best wife for him.

I guess the burning question right at this moment is, which choice should Mukai have made to save her marriage ... insist on being right and continue to demand to her husband to see things from her point of view or just stop being dragged into arguments with her sisters?

Better yet, engage in the arguments with her sisters-in-law whilst her husband was out, handle it and finish it at that!

No need to burden her husband with the details afterwards!

Since it was about survival of the fittest, maybe it would have helped matters had Mukai tried a different tactic ... engage in the verbal warfare with her sister-in-laws; finish with it; then before her husband got home, transform herself into this cheerful, loving, caring wife Mutereri fell in love with.

She would be nothing, but sweet, laughing, smiling, treating her husband to his favourite meal ... a bit hypocritical, but she had to not only survive, right; but thrive !!

As it was, Mutereri was being pulled in two different directions at the same time.

He could not think

He could not breathe

He could not make a decision.

He was suffocating ….

He had to break free !!

Mukai, Arise!

Chapter 5 - Decision time

God will never leave you empty.

He will replace everything you lost.

If He asks you to put something down, its because He wants you to pick up something greater.

"Respect yourself enough to walk away from ANYTHING that no longer serves you, grows you or makes you HAPPY "~Bob Proctor

"I have made my decision ... I am packing my bags, taking my son with me and going back to my parents' home"

Mukai Mukundu Chapfumbu announced this infront of all her in-laws.

There was a hush silence in the room.

Everyone was taken aback.

Who was this woman?

So powerful! So decisive!

Even the four cousin sisters-in-law could not help but marvel at the strength this woman demonstrated!

She called a spade a spade.

She never hid from the truth.

She faced the truth squarely in the face and dealt with it.

She was one never to be paralyzed or immobilized by fear.

Instead she fogged on ahead with fortitude and confidence, shoulders back, chin up!!

Wow!

The instant she announced this, it is said there was a shift in the room.

Typical of human nature, we do not realise what we have until it is gone.

The same was true of this Mutubuki family.

The first one to realise and vocalise this was Mukai's sister-in-law, Gamuchirai.

She stammered

"Eeee ... do you think that is necessary?

Maybe my cousin brother will come back.

Why don't you stay put a little while longer?"

Mukai thought a while about this suggestion and realized that the longer she took to make a firm decision, the harder it would be for her to leave. She could not be a lady in waiting indefinitely.

She needed to get things moving; look after herself and her child.

So, she shook her head and grimly said "No.

My mind is made up.

Mutereri knows where to find me if he ever comes back.

I am out of here. Goodbye "

It was the summer of 1949, 24th January.

Edias Henry Kanamadero Mutubuki was exactly two years old.

The reason for this departure was that exactly a year previously, Mutereri had 'disappeared' ; varnished without a trace.

It is said the couple had had one of their usual rows.

A stalemate had been reached.

Neither one of the parties was willing to move any of the Chase pieces for fear of 'losing' the game of 'he said'; 'she said'!

The next morning, he had left as if he was going to school, but was never heard from again.

That night, Mutereri had not come home ... neither did he pitch the next day after that ... nor the next.

A week passed by and still no word from him.

Mukai and Mutereri 's family were beside themselves with worry.

What could have befallen him?

Was he in some form of trouble?

Was he still alive and if so, where could he be?

If, indeed, he was dead, where was his body?

Mukai solicited the help of a search party who looked everywhere for him ... nearby forests ... combed through the rivers ... climbed mountains and back again!!

NOTHING!!

What were they going to do?

What was SHE going to do?

One month ... two months ... three ... six months ... still no word!!

Once again the bullying and insults began.

People, most especially her four cousin sisters-in-law, taunted and jeered at her that she could not keep a man.

This time, Mukai had no words to use to defend herself. She kept quiet and silently reflected on her life.

Abandonment number four had just reared its ugly head.

This time it was in the name of her husband!

What was she going to do?

Not knowing whether your loved one is still alive or not, is one of the worst tortures ever.

Then something strange happened ...

Seven months after the disappearance of Mutereri, a relative of Mutereri's happened to pass by his home.

He was travelling by bicycle having come from a few kilometres away, a neighbouring district.

Mukai happened to be alone in the house that day.

She had offered him some water to drink and prepared her guest some food to eat.

Then as he was about to take his leave, before climbing back on his bicycle, he said "Oh, and by the way, I bumped into Mutereri yesterday in Mwenezi.

He has changed his name.

He is going by the name of Fedest Sapeta.

He has dropped the Mutereri Mutubuki.

KKK...

I guess he is in hiding!!

Doesn't want you to trace his whereabouts!!"

With that, the relative had laughed again, winked wickedly and was off.

Mukai was left speechless routed to the spot.

So, Mutereri was still alive?!

He was living in the next district under a different name?!!

Mukai sank to the floor and cried her heart out!

Eight months ... nine ... still nothing!

Mutereri did not try to make contact with her.

Ten months ...

Mukai started to think what her next best move was going to be ...

By the twelfth month, she knew.

She would go back to live with her grandmother, Vakudandaya.

She would take her child with her.

Kuitwa gara ndichauya, Mukai Mukundu Chapfumbu akati 'bodo'!!

So, Mukai packed her bags, bid farewell to her in-laws, took her son, and went back to her grandmother's house.

She told herself, Mutereri knows where to find me should he choose to come back.

"So, you are back?"

Vakudandaya uttered the very same words she had asked her own daughter, Matinetsa Kuzipachangwara, more than two decades previously when she too had returned from her marital home when her husband, the king, had died.

Only that, in Mukai 's case, she was not a widow.

No!

Mutereri was still very much alive!

Neither was she a divorced woman.

No!

Mutereri had not asked for a divorce.

He had just bolted like a cow from its pen!

So, what category did she fit into?

Separated?

Not quite, for Mutereri had not asked for a trial separation before he left.

Jilted woman?

Yes, strictly speaking, she fell into this category.

When you come to think of it, this is one of the most painful, most difficult to understand states anyone can ever find themselves in - man or woman - no matter the reason the injured party says to itself.

This is because unlike the other states, there is no sense of closure.

It is one of the most unfairest way anyone can ever subject another person.

It is not right.

It is not fair.

Only a cowardly, self centred, egotistic maniac can ever subject another human being to such humiliation.

Mutereri was a coward. He was not a real man.

Real men face their challenges head on, not cower or hide from them.

Real men make decisions that are mature, well thought out and have the best interests of all persons involved in that relationship; not make decisions that serve only their own selfish interests.

Real men are accountable and take responsibility for their actions, not deny or hide from them.

When things get tough in a relationship, real men get tougher, not weaker.

Mutereri had no right to treat someone else's daughter the way he treated Mukai Mukundu Chapfumbu.

Anyway, being the fighter that she was, once again, Mukai picked up the pieces from where she left off; dusted herself and concentrated on looking after herself, her son and her grandmother.

Her grandmother's place was a bit of a distance for her to commute daily; so she got stuff housing at the school she was teaching.

Since she did not have a nanny to look after her son, she left him under the capable hands of the only person she trusted in this whole wide world, the person who had cared for her in her most vulnerable moments as a six month old baby, her grandmother, Vakudandaya.

Once again, Vakudandaya saw the cycle repeat itself.

First she had looked after her daughter, Matinetsa's daughter, Mukai.

Now she was looking after her grand daughter's son; her great-grandson!

She was speechless!!

But, true to her nature; she lovingly nurtured and raised her great-grandson into a wonderful, centred, happy, intelligent boy.

Edias was nothing like his father.

He was a man unto himself, who knew how to stand up for himself and others.

He was raised to have enormous respect for himself, womenfolk and other humans in society.

Life resumed to normal for Mukai after she had left The Mutubuki household.

Doing what she loved and was good at helped fill her time.

Slowly but surely, she began to heal from her wounds.

As time passed, she was able to actually smile and laugh again.

She quietly and quickly settled into a routine that suited and worked well with her sensible and organized nature.

She would spend a whole week at school, teaching her pupils.

Then spend her weekends at her home with her grandmother and son.

There was so much to do.

She kept busy.

This suited her just fine.

Besides being a great teacher, loving and caring mother and granddaughter, Mukai was also a devout Christian.

Every Sunday she could be seen waking up very early in the morning, taking a bath, dressing up in her Sunday best and cycling to church, which was a bit of a distance from her grandmother's home.

The Dutch Reformed Church.

Not one to talk much, she was an excellent preacher and well known and respected by her fellow parishioners.

She read her Scriptures daily.

Her bible was her constant companion. She prayed daily.

Being the hardworking, diligent, conscientious person that she was, Mukai started to amass a lot of money from her teaching career.

She was sensible and organized.

She used her salary to send her son to school; buy cattle, goats, chickens.

She hired servants who worked in her grandmother's fields.

Year after year, she had a bumper harvest.

In fact, they had such a surplus after accounting for what the family could consume throughout the year, such that she started selling the surplus and made extra cash from that.

Mukai started to really thrive and become famous in her district.

She was a wealthy woman, both in cash and in deed.

She was a generous woman.

Besides looking after her step sister, Vandudzai and step brother, Kota - her mother's children with the man she married after her husband, the king, had died - Mavhoro - Mukai also looked after Mutereri's four cousin sisters' children.

They would approach her and ask her to help them pay school fees for their children.

Mukai would pay.

The Kudandaya household became a house of plenty.

Passersby would purposely choose the path that passed through The Kudandaya household so as to be offered something to eat or drink, for Vakudandaya was said to be generous to a fault!

No one ever left The Kudandaya household empty handed. It was unheard of.

They always left vakagukuchira something!!

Life was smooth and good for years thereafter.

Edias was a bright, intelligent boy.

He attended a Catholic Primary school in Gutu; then went onto attend St Mary's High School - a Catholic Secondary School in the then Salisbury; present day Harare.

He was in Boarding school.

Mukai could afford to send her son to boarding school!!

Wow!!

A single woman working alone could do that!!

She became an inspiration to other girls and women.

It became abundantly clear to them that:

1. There could still be life after divorce or separation - or even after suffering the humiliation ofbeing jilted

2. A woman could still actually go on to thrive after that and be successful in her own right!!

3. It was possible to raise a child all by yourself without the help of a man ...

Not only raise a child, but a BOY child for that matter, who was not only intelligent, but centred, happy and respectful.

4. The importance and value of a support system - support structure.

Grandparents play an important and stabilizing role in their grand children's lives. They are a great and positive influence.

Vakudandaya, played a central support structure in the Matinetsa, Vangana, Tsikai and Njiva lineage.

She was the ROCK, the foundation, a pillar of strength the family needed.

A matriarch.

Hats off to Vakudandaya!

Hats off to all women like Vakudandaya!

Hats off to all the matriarchs of the family in the whole world!

We salute you!!

The first ones to approach Mukai and actually vocalise that they had been wrong were her four cousin sisters-in-law.

One day, several years later, they had paid a visit to her home at the school.

Mukai had been stunned to see them.

It was a Friday afternoon.

School was over for the week and she was about to lock up her house in readiness to cycle to her grandmother's when she saw them.

They had been walking in single file approaching her house.

Mukai had stopped in her tracks and watched as they approached.

'Had something happened?

An illness perhaps ... or a death?' She thought

To her astonishment, they were smiling !!

Upenyu was the first to address her.

"Hallo, there!!

Thought we should surprise you and come visit !!" She laughed and the three laughed too.

For a full minute, Mukai was at a total loss as to what to say. She had just stared at them.

First to reach her was Fungai.

She stopped right infront of her and proceeded to do the unthinkable ... she hugged Mukai!!

Then Gamuchirai had followed suit; then Upenyu.

Last to give her a hug was Ndakarwirwa.

"Oh, well, aren't you going to let us in?!"

Ndakarwirwa had quibbed

Mukai had blinked, got her thoughts together and exclaimed "Of course!!

Please come in.

Where are my manners?"

With that she had proceeded to unlock her door and usher her guests inside.

"We seem to have come at a wrong time.

Looked like you were about to go somewhere?"

Fungai had remarked looking all about her, admiring the furniture, the whole set up.

Everything screamed opulence!

The Razor's Edge !

Bob Proctor in his book entitled 'You Were Born Rich' says the following about this concept and I quote:

'It has often been said the line which separates winning from losing is as fine as a razor's edge and it is.'

Here he was talking about winning in a big way and in all areas of your life.

In his observation over the 60+ years that he has been a Life Coach, there wasn't a big difference among people; there was only a big difference in the things they accomplished.

Mukai Mukundu Chapfumbu was the type of person who fitted into this Razor's Edge concept perfectly.

When others allowed the storms of life to take a toll on them, Mukai used that storm to propel her forward.

Her tenacity, perseverance and courage is what led her to achieve these stupendous achievements.

Mukai had qualities that were very difficult to measure.

She was creative.

Everything she touched turned to gold.

As the four sisters looked about them in awe and wonder, they noticed an eight seater with cushions ... an oak table in the middle with smaller side tables neatly arranged strategically around the seating area ... a 10 seater dining room suite with a display cabinet to the side of the wall ...

Gosh and what was that white metal thing that made a melodious humming sound in the

corner ...?!!

The cousin sisters-in-law would later learn that 'that white metal thing that made a humming sound' was called a paraffin fridge.

The water and drinks that were served from there tasted divine ... so cold as well!!

Wow!!

The kitchen was adorned by this humongous four plate Dover stove with a Dover oven.

The four sisters had never laid eyes on such awesome wonders before.

If they wanted to cook, they had to go to a separate hut that served as a kitchen, light a fire in a pit and cook from there.

The heat and smoke that followed after lighting this fire was more than the eyes could bear. Ko iro ziya!!??

The sweat was unimaginable.

But here was Mukai smartly and easily putting nicely chopped wood inside the burner; lighting the fire and soon the whole stove was hot.

No smoke to contend with.

And the heat did not accost you directly into your face. Instead, it was easily distributed around the Dover !

Mukai filled the kettle, yellow in colour, with water and placed it on one of the plates.

On another, she placed a huge metal pot, yellow in colour as well, which she had filled with water.

She was going to allow it to boil, then prepare mupunga mutsvuku unedovi - boiled rice with peanut butter - a special meal prepared by the Shona.

On the third plate, she had placed another yellow pot, a size smaller than the one she was going to use for boiling the rice.

In this one, she used to boil then fry a roadrunner.

She had gone in her chicken run behind her house and caught one roadrunner - a broiler.

Peeping unashamedly, the cousin sisters-in-law observed that she had more than 50 roadrunners in that chicken run ... 25 Layers and 25 - oh wait - now 24 Broilers!

She had killed the chicken, took boiling water from the kettle, poured it on the now dead roadrunner, soaked it with the hot water and peeled off the feathers.

Surgeon like, she had expertly dissected the chicken, brought out the internal organs, cut and separated them.

The intestines, the gizzard and the liver - she dressed them, washed them thoroughly with water, placed them in a plastic bag and stored them in the freezer in her paraffin fridge.

The rest, she threw away.

She had cleaned the now fully dissected, dressed and cut into pieces chicken, put it in the pot that was already having boiling water, added salt to taste and some oil; then closed it with a lid.

Meanwhile, the rice was already boiling. She reduced the heat for it to cook slowly and eventually simmer.

Whilst all this was cooking on her Dover, Mukai set the table at her dining table.

She covered the table with a white table cloth; placed 5 place mates ... the table was so big; it still had 5 places left!

She had taken out her special China, washed and dried it; then placed each white China plate, cup and saucer on each place mat.

Silver cutlery had also adorned the table.

A silver sugar basin and a white salt and pepper dispenser had also been added as condiments.

Tea with recently baked bread was ready.

All this she did with such proficiency and efficiency, the four sisters could do nothing, but gape.

The four sisters-in-law were treated to the richest, creamiest, great tasting tea they had ever tasted.

And the bread ... wow!!

It smelt great and had the most amazing flavour.

Mukai had also fetched some eggs from her Layers and had fried them.

The sisters had dug in with zest and enthusiasm that put an eight year to shame!!

Handikunakirwa ikoko!!

Waingonzwa 'nhwa' 'nhwa' 'susu' 'susu', kuri kunakirwa nechikafu ikoko.

Kaziya kakati mokoto mokoto on the faces of the sisters.

You see, Mukai may have been an excellent teacher, but she was just as competent in the kitchen!!

She was an excellent chef!!

And a competent homemaker from the looks of it.

Since the cousin sisters-in-law had come in the afternoon and stayed on long after the sun had set; for lighting, Mukai had lit a paraffin lamp.

The four sisters watched mesmerized as she expertly took one lamp, flipped on the glass, light a match and set the wick alight; then close the glass again.

Immediately, the room was filled with a flood of light!

Wow!

The four sisters had never seen such luxury before!!

They were used to walking in the dark at night using only the moon as light.

Wow!!

Dinner was served a few hours after they had had their tea, bread and fried eggs.

Christmas had arrived early that year!

So much food!!

So much light!!

So many soft drinks!!

Wow!

The four sisters vakadya miromo ikaenda paside!!

After they were satiated, Mukai cleaned the table, washed all the dishes and arranged them neatly in a cupboard in the kitchen.

She then wiped and cleaned her Dover stove and swept and mopped her kitchen floor.

Within an hour, her kitchen was back to tip top shape again - clean; everything in its place!

That's how Mukai Mukundu Chapfumbu's mind worked!

A professional through and through.

After this, she washed her hands, neated herself and walked in the Sitting Room to entertain her guests.

"Yuwi!"

Fungai was the first to remark after dinner

"You certainly know your way around the kitchen, muroora!

That tea was out of this world!

One of the tastiest teas I have ever tasted!!"

"And the fried eggs?!

Wow!!

Your Layers lay the best eggs!!

I think you feed them with some special greens ...?!!" Upenyu added

"I particularly loved the bread!!

Freshly made, in your Dover oven, I imagine?" Ndakarwirwa ventured

"Dinner was incredible!!

And you managed to whip all that in such a short space of time?!!

Wow!!

Thank you muroora! Taguta wena!!"

Gamuchirai added

With this, all of them expressed their thanks in unison by clapping in a special way the African Shona do to express deep gratitude, thankfulness and appreciation.

Mukai smiled and said "Muchitendei"

Translation!

"You are welcome"

Funny thing about success, money and wealth ...

Everyone wants to be your friend !!

Everyone wants to be your relative!!

Everyone wants to be associated with you!!

Take these four losers for example!!

They had the audacity and nerve to come to Mukai 's home; eat her food, sit on her sofas and address her as 'muroora' when it was them who caused the rift between her and her husband all those years ago.

Technically speaking, they had no right to call her 'muroora' for their cousin brother had left her years before.

Furthermore, they had no right to take advantage of the goodness of her heart.

"Haa ...

Our cousin brother made the biggest mistake ever by running away from you.

He was wrong. So were we.

We should never have let you go. "

Ndakarwirwa remarked

"Now all this is going to be enjoyed by someone else!!" Gamuchirai glared at Mukai

"So tell us.

Are you seeing anyone?"

Upenyu quizzed Mukai

Mukai is said to have paused a little, thinking then got up and said "If you will now excuse me, I have to go.

When you came I was about to go somewhere."

And with that Mukai Mukundu Chapfumbu is said to have walked into her bedroom, fetched her handbag; walked back into the Sitting Room and ushered the four sisters out of her house; locked it and said "Goodbye"

"But, but its late and dark outside.

We can't go back to our homes now!!."

Fungai remarked

But Mukai retorted

"You are all big girls. You figure it out"

And with that, she jumped on her bicycle and made her way to her grandmother's.

She is said to have reached her grandmother's at midnight.

When she arrived and knocked on her door, Vakudandaya is said to have wondered who that was knocking at her door at such an hour.

When she had opened the door and recognizing her granddaughter she had exclaimed "Hesvu, kwakanaka?!"

Translation!

"Goodness, is everything alright?!"

Mukai did not reply

She just shook her head and got inside the house

Mukai, Arise!

Chapter 6 - Moving on

O Lord, I live in the midst of lions

'Have mercy on me, O God, have mercy, for my soul takes refuge in you; I will find shelter in the shadow of your wings till the disaster has passed.

I will call on God the Most High, on God who has done everything for me: may he send from heaven a savior and put my oppressors to shame.

May God send me his love and faithfulness.

I lie prostrate in the midst of lions that greedily devour people, their teeth are pointed spears and arrows, their tongues, sharpened swords.

Be exalted, O God, above the heavens! Your glory be over all the earth!

They have set a snare for my steps; my soul was bowed down in distress. They dug a pit along my path, but they themselves fell into it.

My heart is steadfast, O God, my heart is steadfast.

I will sing and make music.

Awake my soul, awake, O harp and lyre!

I will wake the dawn.

I will give thanks to you, O Lord, among the peoples, I will sing praise to you among the nations.

For your love reaches to the heavens, and your faithfulness, to the clouds.

Be exalted, O God, above the heavens!

Let your Glory be over all the earth!~Psalm 57 (Christian Community Bible - Catholic Pastoral Edition)

Life was straight forward for Mukai Mukundu Chapfumbu.

It was predictable.

It was safe.

It was tranquil.

No drama like the early years.

No drama like the marital years.

No drama like the early years following the breakdown of her marriage.

Just peace and tranquility.

Mukai thrived.

Mukai shone.

Mukai outdid herself.

For seventeen glorious years, Mukai Mukundu Chapfumbu basked in the glory of her success; in the glory of her son's success; in the glory of her grandmother's happiness.

Then ...

One day, she had a visitor ...

This visitor was not exactly a stranger; but she was a stranger!!

She was not exactly a stranger for she is the one who had given birth to her.

At the same time, she was a stranger for this vessel that had been her gateway onto planet earth had left her to be looked after by another woman when she was barely six months old and had never come back to visit ... until now ... 40 years later!

And the reason for this visit ... her second husband, Mavhoro, had died.

Rather than kugarwa nhaka again, she had refused and opted to go back to her parents' home.

Matinetsa Kuzipachangwara returned to The Kudandaya household in the spring of 1964, exactly 40 years after she had left home.

She now had two grown up children, a 13 year old girl by the name of Vandudzai and a 15 year old boy by the name of Kota.

Mukai's initial response was joy at being reunited with her mother.

Finally she could reignite her relationship with the woman who had given birth to her.

It was a dream come true, indeed!

She also accepted her two step-siblings and treated them like part of the family.

She paid school fees for them both.

Vakudandaya was happy to have her family under one roof at last.

For a while they lived like one big, happy family, until things Mukai didn't like started happening in The Kudandaya household.

Apparently, Matinetsa Kuzipachangwara, her mother, had a tendency to sell Mukai's cattle, goats, maize, groundnuts, chickens, etc without first informing her daughter.

When asked about it and to account for the cash, Matinetsa would become belligerent and aggressive.

She became defensive to try and bully Mukai into not asking any questions so that she could continue with her squander and plunder of her daughter's wealth.

For a time, Mukai tried to speak with her mother and make her see sense, but this only made Matinetsa even more belligerent.

To make matters worse, she started insulting and shouting obscenities at her eldest daughter; accusing her of not giving her enough money.

She would complain to neighbours saying that her daughter did not love her and take care of her.

Initially, Mukai used to ignore her mother's unreasonable requests.

The insults and taunts continued and seemed to get worse.

It is said when Matinetsa started her screams and insults, she would stand infront of the yard for everyone to hear.

She would scream and shout from dawn to dusk.

Passersby would stop and watch this spectacle in total enjoyment.

Some would giggle.

Some would smile

Others would laugh out loud.

Any attempt at restraining her would be met by punches, shoves and more screams.

Life at The Kudandaya household changed from being the peaceful haven people had grown to know, into a place where shouting was the order of the day.

Vakudandaya tried to speak sense into her daughter, but this only added fuel into the already blazing fire.

Mukai put up with her mother's theatrics for two solid years until one day.

Picture this !! ...

A Sunday Service full of parishioners.

The parishioners are not only the local people, but dignitaries who have come from all over the district and beyond.

It's a special day in the Calender of The Dutch Reformed Church

The person presiding over the service at the altar is not their usual Reverend; but The Bishop himself.

He has travelled all the way from Salisbury to preach the Gospel at a local Parish in Gutu.

One of the most famous parishioners and most renowned teachers in the whole of Gutu district is infront of the church.

She has just finished reading a prescribed verse in Scripture.

As she steps down to go and take her seat with other congregants and simultaneously as the Bishop takes his place at the altar, a commotion is heard.

A woman barges into this service.

She is screaming and uttering obscenities.

She scans the whole room full of parishioners until she spots one particular one ...

Mukai !!

She glares at her ... points an accusing finger towards her and screams; glancing first at The Bishop, then at the whole congregation "That's her!!

The ungrateful child whom I gave birth to, who does not look after me!!

Look at me!!

She doesn't even buy me clothes!!"

The woman shouting all these words was Mukai 's own mother, Matinetsa Kuzipachangwara.

She.was.stark.naked!

To say Mukai was embarrassed does not even begin to describe exactly how she felt.

Right at that moment she wished the ground would open and swallow her whole.

How was she going to look at her fellow parishioners again?!

It is said, the Bishop had stopped in mid sentence and stared unbelievably at the charade unfolding right infront of his eyes.

No one spoke.

No one breathed. No one moved.

Mukai remained immobile.

Then 3 minutes later, which felt like eons to Mukai, an usher had the presence of mind to remove his jacket and wrap it around Matinetsa and gently escorted her out of the Church and took her home.

Sunday service continued as normal.

It is said Mukai did not utter a word.

When Sunday service was over, Mukai excused herself.

She did not wait for the scheduled BBQ, but cycled back to The Kudandaya household; packed all her belongings; her son's belongings and her grandmother's belongings; drove all her livestock; took half of that year's harvest and took her son and her grandmother; and it was goodbye Kudandaya household.

They relocated to Mukai 's house at the school.

Within a week, Mukai bought 4 hectares of land near her school; proceeded to build a seven roomed brick under asbestos mansion on it.

She painted it blue.

It had a spacious Sitting Room, separate Dining Room, an impressive kitchen and 4 bedrooms.

One bedroom, the largest, was for her grandmother, Vakudandaya; the second bedroom was for her son, Edias; the third one was hers; the fourth one was for guests.

The house had a massive veranda, which served as a conservatory.

During most weekends, The Mukai household could be seen taking their breakfast or brunch in their conservatory.

Everyone gaped and gawked.

They had never witnessed anything like that before.

The mansion also had an outdoor toilet and bath area at the back.

Mukai fenced the whole 4 hectares.

Noone could get in except through the front gate which was always closed and locked.

Only 3 people had keys to this gate ... herself; her grandmother, Vakudandaya and her son, Edias.

When the mansion was completed, Mukai had a house warming party where she invited all her friends, colleagues at work, and a few close relatives.

Matinetsa was not invited.

Vandudzai and Kota were invited, though.

Mutereri's four cousin sisters were not on the guest list.

Vakudandaya and Edias moved into this mansion - which became known as The Mukai Mansion - exactly a year after that Sunday Service episode.

Mukai never spoke to Matinetsa ever again after that.

Instead she focused with all of her strength and might to continue building and amassing her wealth and looking after both her grandmother and son.

She also continued paying school fees for her two step siblings, but they stayed with their mother at The Kudandaya household.

Mukai never set foot on The Kudandaya household ever again.

If Matinetsa and her children needed provisions, they had strict instructions to approach Vakudandaya, who would look in her dura - storage area - and decide how much to send them.

One of the servants would carry it for them in a chikochikari - ox drawn cart.

If it was cash they needed, Mukai would send her son to bring it to them

The Mukai Mansion flourished.

Mukai had servants who worked inside the house. She had a maid, a chef and a butler.

Mukai had servants who worked around the yard - three gardeners.

One's responsibility was to see to the landscape of the 1acre yard around the house.

The second's responsibility was to tend to the 1 acre vegetable garden at the far back, after the yard.

In these vegetable beds, they grew market gardening vegetables such as rap; kale, cabbage, chomolier; carrots, onions, tomatoes.

There was also an orchard which span an acre.

The third gardener tended exclusively to this.

Fruit trees such as mango, oranges, lemons, avocado pears, peaches, plums, etc. were grown.

Mukai had numerous servants who worked in the fields.

They grew such cash crops as chibage - maize, mapfunde - sorghum, rukweza - rapoko, mupunga mutsvuku - yellow rice, ipwa.

Once again, all roads for passersby passed through The Mukai Mansion.

The only difference was that, this time one could not just barge inside the yard.

They had to knock at the front gate first to be let in.

Mukai, Arise!

Chapter 7 - Miedzo

"As your brother, I think you should marry again!"

Amon demanded

He had popped out of the blue and paid Mukai a visit at her house at the school.

"Step-brother!"

Mukai had corrected acidly

Amon winced but remained silent.

His mouth was set in a grimace and he looked disapprovingly at his STEP - sister.

He had looked around her home with anger, greed and envy at all the obvious opulence that was in this house.

A woman's house at that!!

She had no right to all this wealth!!

It should be HIM who should have been blessed with all this! Not, this 'witch'!

'And there she is sitting there looking at me all high, mighty and taughty like a queen sitting on her throne!!' He fumed

The ancestral spirits had done him a great injustice, indeed!!

They had taken what belonged to him and given it to HER!!

No, there was something wrong with this equation. He did not like it at all.

Amon was beside himself with jealousy and envy. He was seething with rage.

Had he been a snake, he would have been heard hissing from a mile away.

And he could bite!

Oh, he was vicious alright!

Just ask his other siblings, 4 wives and 20 children back at his home!!

They would gladly tell you a story or two about him that was a mile long.

Amon had heard stories about Mukai ever since she was a child.

He had kept a keen and obsessive interest in all her movements.

Some would have called that 'undue attachment'.

He had secretly relished in all her misfortunes; celebrated when he heard she had been jilted by her husband and had come back home.

However, things had started to turn all of a sudden for her.

He started hearing tales of her fame and fortune.

Initially he had not believed them; thinking they were 'tales told by an idiot full of sound and fury'.

But as the tales became more and more over the years, he had summoned the courage to come and see for himself.

He had initially gone to The Mukai mansion but 'Queen' Kudandaya would not let him in!! She had asked him to go see Mukai at her other home at school!!

The old lady hadn't had the decency to even offer him some water to drink, but had spoken behind the safety of her gate!!

The nerve of the woman!

Seething and riling, Amon had marched onto the school. He was now hungry, bitter and resentful!!

He would show this Mukai who was boss!

And she had had the nerve to marry that Mutereri person without first consulting him!!

Who did she think she was?!

All these thoughts had been on Amon's mind.

When he had arrived unannounced at Mukai's doorstep at the school, she had been shocked to see him.

Even though they shared the same father, the king, Mukai had never been close to relatives on

her father's side of the family.

She knew her family background.

Vakudandaya had informed her as she was growing up.

They had, however, never tried to make contact throughout the years.

They went on by their business; and Mukai went on by her business.

They were like oil and water.

The two did not mix.

So, seeing him on her doorstep came as a shock.

Instinct told her that this visit was not a social call. Not by a long shot!

She was sure Amon had something up his sleeve.

She had not ushered him inside her home, but instead, had fetched a bench and a chair and placed them on the veranda.

She had gone onto firmly shut her front door.

This had not gone unnoticed by Amon.

He seethed even more.

So this woman thought she was better than him?!

Well, he was going to show her!!

Mukai was speaking

"As my step-brother, don't you think it is improper and inappropriate that you should be mentioning the subject of marriage to me?

Isn't that what the vatetes - aunts - are there for?!" She retorted

Amon fumed

"How long has that Mutereri of yours been out of the picture?

I only have your best interests at heart.

It's not right and proper for a woman to stay all by herself.

People are talking.

And you only have one child.

Don't you think its time you had other babies?

You are not getting any younger you know.

Your clock is ticking."

Mukai thought to herself

'This man is pathetic!'

She actually felt sorry for him.

So, she laughed and said

"Aaaa ... zvamataura vahanzvadzi ndazvinzwa! I will keep in mind all that you have said "

Amon felt slighted by both Mukai's laugh and her last remark.

He was sure that not only had she seen through him, but that she was also mocking him.

He tasted bile in his mouth.

He had come to ask a favour from her and at this rate he realised that antagonising her was definitely not going to soften her heart towards him.

So, he tried another tactic.

"Oh well.

Suit yourself!"

"I see the ancestral spirits have favoured you greatly!

All this wealth?" Amon started

Mukai remained silent. She just looked at him.

Amon cleared his throat, shifted uncomfortably in his seat, cleared his throat again and said

"Vahanzvadzi muchindiona ndauya kudai, ndine chichemo - sister, I have come with a request ..."

"Yes?"

Mukai said

"I can see that you are a wealthy woman.

Money is not one of your woes.

Since you only have one son and I was blessed with 20 children, my wives and I were talking the other day, and thought it a good idea if some of our children came and stay with you in that mansion of yours.

You can pay their school fees."

Amon finished

Mukai remained silent. Her mind was racing.

Then after a few minutes, she said

"I have heard what you have asked of me.

I will think it over and will get back to you." She said

Amon looked taken aback.

"Can't you make up your mind now?!"

"No. I can't. "

Mukai said and got up

"Now if you could please excuse me?

I have class to attend"

With that, Mukai offered her hand as a sign of farewell.

Amon had no choice but to take the proffered hand and also take his leave.

'What had just happened?!' He asked himself

He felt he had not achieved what he had come for.

And he felt dismissed like a school boy and he did not like the feeling.

The discussion she had had with Amon the other day had disturbed her on two counts:

1. She did not like that he had pitched at her doorstep like that.

She had an odd feeling that her step-brother's resentment and jealousy of her went really deep to the extent that he could be dangerous.

2. What he was asking of her ... to take in some of his children into her home!

She didn't like the idea.

She knew that Amon resented her, so why was he entrusting his children into her care.

Taking in someone under one's care was not something one took lightly.

If anything happened to any of those children whilst they were under her care, how would she be able to explain it to their father?

Would he be able to listen to reason?

Something told her, no.

This sounded more of a trap than anything.

Amon was up to something.

It was clear.

Taking in his children was out of the question.

It was too much of a big risk.

She had had enough drama in her life to last her a lifetime. She did not need to add more.

So, how was she going to turn him down without aggravating him further ... without making herself look like a villain?!ჰ

Mukai thought some more.

Then, ting!!!

Eureka!!

An idea had suddenly popped into her mind ...

"The reason I called you here is to accept your proposal " Mukai began

To say that Amon had grinned from ear to ear is a great understatement ever told.

He was so happy, his hands literally shook!

Now his chance of slowly percolating into this 'witch's' life was inches away!!

With his children firmly anchored in this place, he would slowly, but surely start to prise away Mukai 's tentacles from this place.

He gave himself a year.

He could see himself moving in, taking over and eventually throwing Mukai out of this place, along with her beloved son and that grandmother of hers!

Afterall, all this belonged to him !!

He smiled as he visualized moving in with his family.

A family as big as his needed a place as big and spacious as this.

Who knows, with any luck, maybe he would take on a fifth wife!

That Sharai girl would fit perfectly as his next acquisition!

Amon was day dreaming

Oops, Mukai was speaking

"BUT I have a proposal of my own" Mukai held out a steadying hand

Amon and the 10 children he had brought stopped dead in their tracks.

They sensed that more was coming.

"As you can see, I have acres upon acres of land here that need ploughing, tilling, planting, tending and eventually, harvesting.

I would also need manpower that would cart the produce to the market when the crop is ready." Mukai spoke

Amon and his children looked confused for a minute as they could not get her drift.

Mukai realised their plight, smiled and said "Ok, let me rephrase.

What I am offering is this ....

I would gladly take in your 10 children, live with them under the same roof as me and I pay school fees for them under FOUR conditions:

1. In return they will work in these fields everyday, except Sunday, from 3am until 6am; break offsince they will need to get ready for school; attend school from 7am until 4pm; come back home straight after school and go straight to the fields to resume work; knock off around 7pm when there is no longer day light.

2. They will not live in my house, per se, but in the servant's quarters.

3. I will only start paying fees after I am satisfied that they are willing and committed to ourarrangement.

4. Should they breach any of our agreement, this Verbal Contract becomes null and void.

I will not want to see either you or any of your children approaching me again and addressing the same subject.

As you can see, I do not have enough space in my own house as all bedrooms are taken. They already have owners.

But I have plenty of space at the Servant's Quarters " Mukai finished, smiling

Absolute silence followed.

To say Amon was stunned, is because we do not have a better word in the English dictionary to describe how shocked he was.

'This woman!'

Is the only phrase that kept repeating in his mind like a broken record Amon looked disbelievingly, first at his step-sister, then at his 10 children.

"You are joking, right?!

Tell me it's a prank and I'll be the first one to burst out laughing!"

Amon blurted

Mukai looked him squarely and fully in the eye and said "No.

Its not a joke, 'brother'! I am serious "

Again, there was stunned silence.

Then ...

"You mean you want my kids to come and work for you in return for you to provide board, lodgings and paying school fees for them?" Amon's voice was low and threatening

"If you put it that way, yes"

Mukai challenged

"But, but ... my children are your children ...?!" Amon hesitated

"Exactly!

If you notice,'brother', there are no free rides in The Mukai mansion.

Everyone pitches in" Mukai said cooly

Amon took a deep breath.

He could see his dream slowly fade away ... unless ...

"One minute ..."

He said and pulled his pack to one side

The troupe was involved in a heated discussion.

They were speaking in hushed tones, so Mukai's sharp ears could not pick out what was actually being said between the eleven.

From the way he was flinging his arms about, Amon was insisting on something; whilst the kids were insisting on something else.

Five minutes later, they were back.

"Ok.

Its settled.

We agree to your terms.

When can they move in?" Amon asked

"Right now, if they want."

Mukai shrugged

Amon turned to his children and said "Boys, you heard the lady!

Let her escort you to your living quarters. I will be seeing you!"

With that he made to take his leave.

"You don't want to see where your kids will be staying from now on?"

Mukai had been surprised

Amon shook his head, turned and without a backward glance, walked away.

Mukai watched him leave.

So did his children.

The forlorn look on their faces made Mukai's heart ache.

'What kind of monster is this?'

She wondered

For a full minute she considered reconsidering the Verbal Contract that she had just entered with her step-brother.

But when she remembered the expression on his face when she had initially informed him that she was going to accept his offer, she shivered.

At that moment, she decided to follow through with the Contract.

"What?

How many did you say have left today?"

Mukai asked the foreman

"Three, Mam"

He announced

"That makes a total of eight in the last two months!"

Mukai shook her head

The foreman chuckled and quibbed

"Apparently, hard work is not for everybody, Mam!!"

Mukai just shook her head again.

'Apparently, hard work was not everybody's cup of tea, indeed!' Mukai thought to herself as she walked back to the main house.

In the last two months, Amon's children had found the schedule at The Mukai mansion, hard to bear.

They had moaned and groaned and complained throughout.

They could not cope with the early hours and the long hours of the day.

None of them could wake up at 3am, as stipulated in the verbal agreement between herself and their father, so the Foreman had extended their shift to end at 8 in the evening.

This had not gone on well with any of the children.

They found work in the fields laborious, hard, dull and boring.

They hated school with a passion and found it exhausting and a complete waste of time.

'Go to school and get an education ..?!!

What for?!

I'd rather just sleep the whole day.

Better!

But call me when lunch is ready!!'

'Earn my keep?!

What for?!

I am entitled to you giving me what I want without me working for it first!!'

'Clean my room?!

What for?!

Isn't that what servants are there for?!'

So, one by one, they had sneaked back to their father's house.

Only two were left.

Mukai promised herself that if these two that were left could last another month, then they would have passed the litmus test and she would ease their work load and move them to live inside the main house.

She had no problem letting them occupy the guest room.

But would you believe ... exactly two days before the third month was to be over, these two also disappeared after school.

They never returned to The Mukai mansion!

"And then they were none!!"

Mukai laughed when her grandmother broke the news that weekend when she came back from school.

"Too bad!"

Vakudandaya had shaken her head

"And to think that they had stuck it out for this long, only to give up at the finish line!"

"Oh, well, 'all that's well, ends well !!'

Mukai quoted Shakespeare

"Will you still pay their school fees?"

Vakudandaya asked

"No, granny.

I won't.

They breached their side of the Contract, so that makes our Contract null and void " Mukai added grimly

Vakudandaya shook her head and continued with her knitting.

She was always busy; never idle.

She used to always say

'An idle mind is the devil's workshop '

Mukai, Arise!

Chapter 8 - Chinokura chinokotama

'Chinokura chinokotama musoro wegudo chave chinokoro'

Edias thrived at St Mary's High School in Salisbury, graduated with honours and went on to enrol at Umtali Teachers College; present day Mutare Teachers College in 1968.

Like his mother, he trained as a teacher - a secondary school teacher.

During this era in Rhodesia, present day Zimbabwe, the choices of professions a black African could do were limited.

You could either train as a nurse, a policeman/ policewoman or as a teacher.

Anything else like Medical Doctor, Quantity Surveyor, Engineer, Accountant, Journalist, etc was reserved for the white folk.

That was the face of colonialism in Southern Africa.

And that was the era in which Edias was born and grew up in.

At College, he met and fell in love with this beautiful, driven, focused, determined young woman from Enkeldorn, present day Chivhu.

Never in his life had he met anyone as strong, as clear headed, as hard working and as devout as this lady.

Her name ... Laurentia Eunah Chambiwa.

Unlike him who was majoring in the Arts like English and Philosophy; this girl was majoring in the Sciences.

She was chikwapuro in Mathematics, Biology and Chemistry.

Laurentia Eunah came from a mixed culture.

Her father was Zulu from Natal, Durban, South Africa.

He had arrived in Rhodesia with his only relative, his sister, Bessina.

Elijah and Bessina had been part of the Pioneer Column that emanated from Bechuanaland.

History has it that after the Dingane fiasco, the Zulu tribe was in disarray.

Laurentia's bloodline ended up in the employ of a British White family.

When the Pioneer Column started, it is said Laurentia 's grandparents put their two children under the care of a British white family that was travelling to Mashonaland.

It is said the grandparents felt that Mashonaland was the 'greener pastures' their children would potentially benefit from.

So, Laurentia's father, Elijah, and his sister Bessina, hitched a ride on one of the ox drawn caravans and started their long journey from Macloutsie to initially, Matabeleland; then proceeded to Mashonaland.

It is said that when Elijah and his sister finally arrived with the Column at Fort Salisbury, they were given arable land and settled in Enkeldorn (present day Chivhu).

Elijah got a job as an ambulance driver.

He used to ply the streets of Redcliff, present day Kwekwe.

Laurentia's mother, Esnath Elizabeth Chikanyira was a local.

She came from The Chivhu area.

She was the youngest child in a family of three girls.

Laurentia's parents had passed on whilst she was still in school.

She had an elder sister, Shirley and two younger brothers, Lawrence Liquor and Coban.

The two hit it off.

It was an exciting time for these two.

They enjoyed a wide group of friends. Socialites, one would call them.

Edias' best friend was this young, vibrant, vivacious and influential Catholic Priest by the name of Father Jakata.

They went everywhere together.

Did everything together. They were inseparable.

Laurentia's best friend was Betsero. She was just as devout.

Every Sunday you would find them looking smart and elegant, holding their handbags in one hand and their Bibles in another, quickly making their way to a nearby Cathedral - Holy Trinity Catholic Cathedral.

Laurentia and Edias dated throughout College and so it came as no surprise when Edias popped the question soon after graduation.

Laurentia said 'YES'.

Mukai Mukundu Chapfumbu was overjoyed.

Now she had a companion, a confidante, a helper, a friend - a daughter!!

Her family had just expanded and she basked in the glory of it.

As is custom in the African Shona culture, when a boy child is about to get married, he informs his father and all his relatives.

They are the ones who are expected to take the lead during the lobola process and preside over the matters.

With this in mind, Edias approached his father, Mutereri Sapeta.

True to his nature, Mutereri was inept.

Instead of pulling up his socks and get things moving, he dilly-dallied, bit about the bush, and took Edias in circles.

Bottom line, in the end, Mukai had to step in.

She organized the entourage that was to go to The Chambiwa family; gave Edias the required cash plus cattle and goats demanded during the Lobola.

The proceedings went well.

The Chambiwa/ Pedzisa family was happy.

They agreed that the Church Wedding could take place the following year.

19th September 1971, Edias and Laurentia said "I DO!"

The younger daughter of Elijah Chambiwa and Esnath Elizabeth Chikanyira Chambiwa married Edias Henry Kanamadero Mutubuki at Serima, Gutu.

Presiding over the wedding was none other than Edias' best friend, Father Jakata.

Betsero, of course, was the Maid of Honour.

A moving and touching ceremony it was!

Mukai Mukundu Chapfumbu was the happiest Mother-In-Law ... beaming from ear to ear ...

looking drop dead gorgeous in a brand new three piece suit, high heels and clutching her brand new handbag.

God is good, indeed!!

Life as an in-law; mother-in-law, was a different cattle of fish for Mukai, but she took it all in its stride.

To her, Laurentia was more than just a daughter-in-law.

She was her daughter; her closest friend; an extension of her.

Her life now revolved around her work, her home and her son's home.

When Laurentia subsequently became with child and her eldest granddaughter was born, Mukai was on cloud nine!

The Lord had blessed her family indeed. It was growing!!

When the second and third granddaughters were added to the mix, Mukai now had no words.

All she did was praise the Lord.

Then the war hit!

It was 1976 ...

Umtali became a warzone ... Gutu became a place where instead of finding refuge in your own home, you had to run away from the soldiers and hide in bushes and caves.

It was no longer safe.

Ian Smith's regime had become so fierce and so vicious, it was now terrorizing the masses in the rural areas.

Mukai found herself stuck between a rock and a hard place.

There were the Rhodesian forces of Ian Smith on one hand; and the Guerrilla Fighters of Robert Mugabe, on the other.

The game play at the time was, RUN away from the Rhodesian forces if you valued your life AND APPEASE the Guerrilla Fighters if you valued your life.

It was a delicate balance that needed to be managed with brevity, courage and a tenacious will to survive and ultimately, thrive.

The Guerrilla Fighters were feared and revered.

Feared for they could be ruthless.

Revered because they were war heroes fighting for the liberation of the country.

Anyone accused of 'witchcraft' was killed in the most cruel way.

Most people who lived to tell the tale will never forget the loud cries and shrieks of the many men and women tortured and killed for this 'crime'.

Pungwe!!

They used to call it.

Pungwe is a Shona word for 'gathering' held specially at night. Its a special type of vigil.

Whereas with a normal vigil, the church devouts sing and pray the whole night through; at a Pungwe, the attendees, who included the Guerrilla Fighters and the local folk in that district, would be given a lecture by the Guerrilla Fighters as to why they were fighting, who they were fighting and who their Commander-in-Chief was.

This would be followed by a series of inquisitions as to who, among the attendees, was a 'mutengesi' - sell out.

A sell out was anyone who supported the Rhodesian forces.

Anyone identified as a 'sell out' would be dragged, kicking and screaming, to the middle of the gathering ... beaten till they could no longer speak, move, even see.

The beatings were so severe and tortuous; meant to send a clear message and warning to anyone else who dared betray them that this would be the fate that awaited them should they ever dare do the same thing.

The only problem with this type of investigation and punishment was that 'witch hunting' became the order of the day.

If the lady next door was jealousy or envious of the other lady next door, she would accuse her of being a 'witch' when in truth she wasn't, and this terrible fate would befall her.

As a result, many innocent people were wrongfully tortured and killed.

Mukai found herself thrust right in the middle of this fiasco.

When the war hit in Gutu, schools closed; people lost their source of wealth ... cattle, goats, chickens, crop.

People lost their homes as they were plundered, looted and sometimes burnt to the ground by the Rhodesian forces.

Girls and women were vandalized, molested, raped, maimed, even killed in the chaos and mayhem that ensued.

Many women got pregnant and delivered babies the identity of the fathers remained anonymous to this day.

It was really a frightening time.

So much uncertainty

So much suffering

So much blood shed

Mukai 's life now revolved around going to the fields to till the land ... run away from The Rhodesian forces if she saw her fellow neighbours doing the same ... hide in the bush carrying her youngest granddaughter at the time, on her back; at the same time, clutching the hand of her eldest granddaughter.

Her daughter-in-law would have sprinted on ahead to a much further forest with her second daughter in hot pursuit.

Her son was studying in a land far far away - mhiri kwemakungwa, she used to brag.

Edias was studying abroad in The UK at Bristol University. He was doing his Bachelor's Degree

"Tinofara isu! Tinofara isu!"

Her youngest granddaughter, Gamuchirai, sang happily and loudly on the back of her beloved grandmother.

"Shhhh ..."

Mukai whispered trying to quieten her granddaughter

Just then, a group of about 10 to 15 Rhodesian forces passed by.

They looked fierce and frightening in their camouflage uniforms, matching caps and black boots.

They walked in single file looking this way and that.

They were carrying FN rifles and rounds of spare bullets around their shoulders.

When they trudged on in the tall grass, their boots made a deafening sound.

Mukai and her two grandchildren froze.

They dared not breathe.

Even the 6 month old Gamuchirai who had been singing her cares away just a few minutes before, sensed danger and remained immobile on her grandmother's back.

Luckily the forces did not notice them and walked on.

Mukai and her grandchildren remained in hiding till the sun went down.

Then when they saw their neighbours coming out of their hiding places, they followed suite.

They then walked home.

The sun had set.

Her daughter-in-law and second granddaughter arrived much later in the evening that night.

About a week after this episode, Mukai, her daughter-in-law plus their servants were working inside the yard ... sweeping, mowing, watering the plants, etc, when all of a sudden, a giant of a man just appeared by their gate.

He was wearing a brown uniform, brown cap and clad in thick army boots.

As if his height and manner was not scary and menacing enough, he was carrying a rifle - an AK47 - and spare bullets around his shoulders.

This Goliath of a man had appeared without warning and from nowhere such that Mukai and her family had been startled.

He stood towering the gate.

From the looks of it, he had been standing by the gate watching them for a while before they had seen him.

So busy were they in their tasks, they hadn't noticed him.

When they finally did, Mukai and her family had been so startled and afraid they had just stared at him without uttering a word.

"Well, aren't you going to let me in?!" The Guerrilla Fighter bellowed

He had this loud, booming voice that matched his height.

Mukai shivered, placed a protective hand towards her family and moved forward.

Nervously she smiled and said

"Ah ... welcome, Comrade.

My apologies.

So engrossed were we in our work, we didn't see you standing there."

Then reaching the gate, she unlocked it, opened and said "Please come in, sir"

The Comrade walked through the gate and closed it behind him.

He smiled displaying white perfectly even teeth and said "Its good to see people who still take their work seriously. My name is Comrade Hondo.

Pamberi nechimurenga! - Forward with the liberation of our people!"

He followed his introduction with the salute the Guerrilla Fighters used to make as a preface to anything they did.

Mukai and her family stood at attention, raised their fists in the air, just the way Comrade Hondo had just done, as was the expected salute and responded in their loudest voices "Pamberi !! - Forward !!"

"Can you please give me a seat and a drink of water?"

He asked

"Of course."

Mukai said

Turning to one of the servants, Laurentia said

"Ruramisai, please fetch this gentleman some water.

Abamunini Chenje, please get this gentleman a bench "

Within minutes the gentleman was seated and sipping his water.

After he had his fill he said

"So, what is the name of this household?"

Mukai said

"This is The Mutubuki household"

"I see.

And where is the man of the house?"

The gentleman bellowed scratching his knee absently.

"My dad vari mhiri kwemakungwa!"

Mukai 's second granddaughter, Chandirekera Sarah, announced proudly

"Shhh !!"

Laurentia chided her daughter quietly and pulled her away.

The rest of the entourage followed.

Only Mukai was left chatting with the gentleman.

He was seated on the bench.

She was seated on a chair.

They were seated in the shade under a mulberry tree.

"Mhiri kwemakungwa, eh?!

May I know where exactly?"

The gentleman asked

"My son is studying at a university in England "

Mukai revealed Her heart was thumping

"England?!

Did you say, ENGLAND?!"

The gentleman bellowed, his eyes popping out with rage and shifting towards her in a threatening manner.

"Yes, Comrade.

Is there anything wrong with that?"

Mukai spoke nervously fiddling with her fingers

"Is there anything wrong with that?!"

He mimicked her

"OF COURSE THERE IS something wrong with that!!

Mwana wenyu arikudyidzana nevapambe vepfumi!!

Your son is in cohorts with the enemy !!

How do you think that makes me feel ... me fighting here in the bush for our country and him traipsing, befriending and enjoying himself in luxury rubbing shoulders with the very people who are colonizing us and making our lives a living hell !!?

He should be joining hands with me and going to fight in the bush !!"

The gentleman had now stood up and glaring at the older woman who was now shaking like a leaf but trying desperately not to show it.

She could easily be his mother, he was thinking to himself.

Mukai smiled and said "Comrade.

There are many ways of 'fighting' a system that one doesn't like.

Some, like you, take up arms, go into the bush and actually fire bullets at the enemy in order to try and put pressure on him to stop the injustices.

Others, like my son, take up arms in the form of furthering their education, mix and mingle with the enemy in order to learn more about them, hence, know how best to run this country after we win the war.

So, Comrade, I salute you and all the men and women who are sacrificing their lives everyday in order to make our life safer and bring justice to every person in this country regardless of race, gender, creed."

Then mastering all her courage, Mukai Mukundu Chapfumbu leapt to her feet and chanted

"Pamberi neChimurenga !"

holding up her fist in the air as was the expected gesture

"Pamberi!"

The gentleman lept to his feet as well

"Pamberi negidi!" Mukai chanted

"Pamberi !"

The gentleman responded

"Vakomana, vasikana ... Zimbabwe ... maguerilla mumakomo, haiwa taimhanyamhanya takabereka sabhu tichidzingirira Zimbabwe ..."

Mukai started singing and dancing to this popular war song.

Haaa ... it is said the Comrade was so overjoyed, he threw his weapons on the ground and responded to the song, singing, clapping and dancing.

Kakuruva kakati mokoto mokoto !!

Laurentia, who had been peeping nervously concerned about her mother-in-law's safety came running and when she witnessed this show, started ululating, and joined in the singing and dancing!!

The servants came too and joined in the show!! What a day they had!

That song was followed by another; then another!!

It is said they danced so much, rukuruva rukati pano hatisaririri , ko iro ziya ... hanzi kuti mokoto mokoto!!

It is said the gentleman smiled and laughed so much by the time he left a few hours later totally full and satiated what with a belly full of a delicious roadrunner that had been boiled, fried and seasoned along with mupunga unedovi plus tomato and onion soup yaibwinya bwinya; was the best of friends with Mukai.

Pamberi nechimurenga !!

Mukai, Arise!

Chapter 9 - Freedom?

18th April 1980!!

The year Zimbabwe finally got its independence!!

Mukai remembers this day like it was yesterday!!

Rhodesia changed its name to Zimbabwe.

After decades upon decades of fighting and so much blood shed!

So much joy in the streets ... people running ... celebrating ... singing ... dancing ... clapping ... ululating ... beating drums ... blowing trumpets ... !!

Men, women, girls and boys running across the streets of Gweru, Harare, Mutare, Masvingo, Chivhu ... the whole country.

Mukai had never witnessed so much joy expressed by millions of people as a single unit!

Electric!

It truly is terrific the amount of positive energy that can be harnessed by a group of people committed towards a common goal!!

There is nothing like it!!

Haa ... life was good!!

Finally, God had answered Zimbabweans prayer.

Ceasefire!!

The most beautiful words in the English vocabulary.

Peace!

Wow!

That word, peace ... so valuable, so precious, so necessary in society; yet usually taken for granted!

Peace!

Now there would be peace in people's hearts.

Now there would be peace in people's souls Now there would be peace in people's families

Healing!

People needed to heal from the wounds caused by the atrocities of the war.

People needed to heal from the injuries and injustices of the war.

People needed to heal from the emotional and physical scars incurred during the war.

Forgiveness!

People needed to forgive themselves for the atrocities and injustices they had committed to others during the war.

People needed to forgive others for the crimes and horrors they caused them during the war.

People needed to forgive if they were to be able to move on and go onto thrive in a new Zimbabwe.

And with peace and justice, meant no more discrimination on the basis of race, gender, creed.

This is the era Mukai Mukundu Chapfumbu's three granddaughters, Mukai Henrieta; Chandirekera Sarah and Gamuchirai grew up in.

Her granddaughters could now attend schools of their choice; go to any hospital of choice, live in residential areas they chose, take up career opportunities of their choice!

No more restrictions!

No more discrimination! No more segregation!

Now that was true freedom !!

Edias' graduation at Bristol University coincided with Zimbabwe's independence.

He flew back to Zimbabwe in 1980 and settled with his family in Mkoba, Gweru, Village 11 at Number 5480

Her two granddaughters, Mukai Henrieta and Chandirekera Sarah enrolled at St Paul's Primary School.

It was walking distance from home.

So every morning, the two sisters could be seen wearing their navy green uniforms, knee length white socks and brown shoes, carrying their school bags headed to school.

Edias had gotten a job at Gweru Teacher's College as a Lecturer.

Laurentia had enrolled at Mambo High School as a teacher.

Life for her son and his family was going on well.

Mukai was still in Gutu.

But she was now retired.

Gweru and Gutu were too far away from each other, Mukai found herself missing her family.

Fate favors fortune.

It favors the prepared.

As luck would have it, white people in the country were dispensing their properties and relocating to South Africa.

1 year after independence, it happened that one white man, by the name of Gladhill was selling his piece of land - 5 hectares - at No. 13 Laverton Estate, Claremont Road, Shurugwi Road, Daylesford, Gweru.

Edias ceased that opportunity and bought that piece of land for his mother.

It was a three bedroom brick under tile home with a borehole.

Edias and his family were staying in one of the Staff Accommodation at Fletcher High School.

Edias was still lecturing at Gweru Teacher's College, but Laurentia had transferred to Fletcher High School.

The three granddaughters had also transferred schools.

They were now learning at Senga Primary School.

Mukai came to view the No. 13 Laverton Estate, Claremont Road, Shurugwi Road property.

She refused to move in citing it was too porsche for her.

A year later, again as luck would have it, another white man by the name of Ferreira was selling 400 hectares of farm land at No. 57A Umsungwe Block, Sangari Farm, 20 km outside Gweru.

He was in a hurry to leave the country and join his grown up son in South Africa.

So he was selling this property for a song.

Edias knew how to strike whilst the iron was hot, so he bought the property.

The property had a brick under metal roof house ... 3 bedrooms ... three lounges ... a tea room ... one bathroom.

The source of lighting and heating was gas.

It had a state of the art borehole, a massive and rich orchard ... lush vegetation and greenery to simply die for ... wildlife ... wild fruit ...

As if that was not enough, it had a huge mountain!!

This was the perfect location for Mukai Mukumbu Chapfumbu to finally retire at.

So, in the spring of 1982, Mukai bade 'bye bye' to Gutu, packed all her belongings and said 'hallo' Gweru!!

Finally she could rest.

She could see her family during weekends when they visited.

Mukai had the services of a maid, a head rancher and servants who worked in the fields.

Technology had moved up a notch !

She had a telephone inside the house!!

Now at the touch of a button, she could make contact with anyone she desired.

Meanwhile, the family was growing.

In 1981, Mukai's fourth granddaughter, Fungai, was born.

3 years later, in 1984, her fifth, Tinotenda, followed.

3 years later, in 1987, her sixth granddaughter, Ropafadzo, was born, completing the full picture of her grandchildren.
Life proceeded with its ups and downs.

Sometimes one was on top, at other times, one was at rock bottom.

Sometimes one was happy, at other times one was sad.

Sometimes one was strong for others, at other times, others were strong for you.

That's life.

Mukai took it in its stride.

Besides her son being her source of joy, her granddaughters also proved to be her source of pride and joy.

The six granddaughters excelled in school.

All the six girls graduated with honours in High School and went onto enrol at various universities across the globe.

All the six girls have Masters Degrees

Now in Mukai 's family she had Quantity Surveyors; Accountants; Civil Engineers; Journalists and Business Administration specialists.

God continued being gracious to Mukai Mukumbu Chapfumbu's bloodline.

Mukai, Arise!

Chapter 10 - The Mutereri saga

The Mutereri saga

"Sometimes you have to play the role of a fool to fool the fool who thinks they are fooling you"

Apparently when Mutereri left Mukai Mukundu Chapfumbu in Nemataruse, Gutu, he headed straight into Nuanetsi, present day Mwenezi.

He wanted to get as far away from Mukai and his sisters as possible.

And he didn't want them to track him down, so he changed his name from Mutereri Mutubuki, to Fedest Sapeta.

He was sure that with a name like Fedest Sapeta, no one would ever be able to make the link.

He got a job as a teacher at a nearby school.

Life was good.

He wanted a fresh start.

He could not cope married to Mukai.

She was far too powerful and suffocated him.

She was also far too intelligent and always managed to see through him, meaning he could hardly get away with anything.

Being a strong and powerful woman, she acted like a 'lioness' both at work and at home.

If she had acted like a 'kitten' at home, then maybe their marriage may have had a chance.

She was a lionness and roared like one.

She did not know the art of negotiation.

He was of the Soko tribe.

They preferred diplomacy as a form of negotiation, not out right war.

So, he had bolted.

Initially, it was in an attempt to clear his head and device the best way forward, but as one week drew into two, then a month ... he began to like and love his new life more.

Finally he could breathe!

Finally he could express his opinion and someone listened!

Finally he could be his own man!

No more controlling women in the form of his cousin sisters!

Now he could make his own decisions.

Phew!

'What about your son, Edias?

Don't you want a relationship with him?' A voice said

But he quashed that voice.

He will deal with it later.

A year passed.

He had heard through the grapevine that Mukai had arranged a search party to look for him a week after he had gone missing.

So she cared!Ӟ

'Anyway', he shrugged his shoulders Another year passed.

He was enjoying his 'bachelorhood'

Noone knew that he was a married man posing under a different pseudonym.

Women fell at his feet.

He was handsome, eligible, intelligent, generous, well spoken.

To top it off, he was a brilliant teacher.

Everyone had tremendous respect for him.

If only they knew his secret!

Two years later, he heard through the grapevine again, that Mukai had left their matrimonial home and gone back to live with her grandmother, Vakudandaya.

He had mixed feelings about this.

On one hand, he felt 'dumped' and 'discarded'.

He would have liked it had she stayed on.

It would have raised his ego had she stayed on; meaning she still cared enough and still hoped he would someday return.

Returning to her grandmother's home meant that she had moved on.

That was not a good sign.

This woman was stronger and more independent than he had earlier realized.

On another, he felt relieved as she had made her mind up for the both of them.

Now he could live without the guilt.

Now he could move on.

So, he married this woman he had been seeing for the last year.

Her name was Fadzai Munemo.

She was the exact opposite of Mukai Mukundu Chapfumbu.

Whereas Mukai was well educated and a woman of independent means, Fadzai had ended her formal education in Grade 1.

She could barely read, let alone write.

Whereas Mukai was fiesty, hot tempered and spoke her mind; Fadzai was placid, even tempered and rarely said a word.

He used to joke and call her his 'miss too goody shoes'

Whereas Mukai was very hard working, rarely sat down, always busy with this project or that project; Fadzai was lazy.

You actually had to snap at her to get a cup of water to drink.

Whereas Mukai was an excellent chef and homemaker, organized; Fadzai was disorganised, careless and her sense of hygiene left a lot to be desired.

These qualities and more, are the reasons Mutereri married Fadzai in the first place and seven years later, the exact reasons he divorced her - wait! - he didn't 'divorce' her!

No!

He just jilted her!

In the exact manner in which he had jilted Mukai Mukundu Chapfumbu.

At least this time he had the staying power to last him seven years with one woman; three children later - Seretse, Enesia, Nyasha Cleopas.

It is said one day, seven years into his second marriage, Mutereri just did not come back home.

Fadzai tried to look for him, but he had varnished without a trace.

Noone knew where he had gone.

As she was frantically looking for him, that is when she got wind that infact, Mutereri was still married to a now famous and accomplished lady by the name of Mukai Mukundu Chapfumbu of Maregedze Primary School in Gutu.

'What?!'

She could have fainted

It is said Fadzai paid Mukai a visit, in tears and going "Vakoma, I didn't know that Mutereri is married !!

Now he has jilted me the way he did you all those years ago.

At least you have a career and can look after yourself and your son.

I don't and have three children to look after!

Tell me, what am I going to do?"

Mukai is said to have comforted the poor woman saying "There!

There!

Don't cry.

Maybe he will come back"

But Mutereri did not come back.

Neither did he make contact with his three children.

It was 'Hasta la vista Fadzai', 'hasta la vista my three children'.

You can fend for yourselves!

Vakaonana havashayani !!

It is said Fadzai was in such a terrible financial state that she struggled to feed her three children, let alone, send them to school and had to come begging Mukai to help her with the school fees.

Mukai paid the three kids school fees until they graduated from Secondary school.

'I just wanna be a chameleon so that I can be INVISIBLE in VISIBLE'~ Podduturi Vijayasri

The conman was on the hunt again !!

He was ready to strike!

Had he been a cobra, he would have been a venomous, poisonous snake.

This time he did not change his name.

He was sure Fadzai was too 'stupid' to track him down.

This time he disappeared into Harare.

He got a job as a teacher in Highfields.

He married this woman who was described as 'exceptionally beautiful'.

She could have been a model.

Marjory Ganda was her name.

Marjory was said to be extremely fair - very light in complexion,10 years Mutereri's junior, clever, outgoing, knew the way of the world, had her sights very far in the world, materialistic ... oh, did I say clever?!!

Yes, Marjory was clever.

The pair had three children ... Maema, Shepherd and Kwaedza Grace

It is said Marjory had been born and brought up in Harare.

She was young, a breath of fresh air and full of life.

Mutereri fell head over heels in love with this young girl and showered her with gifts to win her heart.

For the first time in his life, he felt like a young man again.

He felt he could conquer the world.

He bought a house in Highfields.

Life was good.

He managed to forget about his two previous marriages with its four children and concentrated on looking after these three .

Then lightning struck!!

There is a saying in Shona that goes

'Dindingwe rinonaka parinokweva rimwe, kana iro rokwevewa, roti mavara angu azare ivhu!'

Translation!

Find a Shona speaking Zimbabwean and ask them!!

Seven years into the marriage, Marjory varnished without a trace!

It is said, she just up and left one day without leaving a forwarding address!

It is said, Mutereri had been home that day as it was a Saturday.

Marjory had murmured something about going to the shops to buy some milk.

The kids were playing in the front yard.

Mutereri was reading his morning paper and sipping his tea.

He is said to have absently murmured a response without even looking up.

Marjory had opened the gate and without a backward glance, had walked away!

Walked away from Mutereri; walked away from her three children; walked away from her life; never to be heard from again.

When one hour ... then two ... then three hours had passed and still Marjory had not returned, Mutereri became worried.

Where could she be?

"Father, where is Mummy?"

5 year old Maema asked

"I don't know"

Mutereri had responded

"Shouldn't she be back by now?"

Shepherd asked, already perceptive for a 4 year old

"Yes, she should "

Mutereri was now frowning

Little Grace started to cry. "I want my Mummy!! And I want my milk!"

Mutereri ran to the little girl and tried to comfort her.

The instant the others heard their baby sister crying, they too started to cry.

It was like a scene from a nursery show.

Mutereri tried to comfort one child, but the instant he left this one; the other one started yelping.

He did not know what to do.

After 10 frustrating minutes, Mutereri is said to have sunk to the floor and wept like a baby.

24 hours later, he had gone to the police and filed a missing persons' report.

The police were sure they would find her.

'Poor lad.

Left with three young toddlers all below the age of 6!!'

The police looked at one another and shook their heads.

One month ... two ... three... but Marjory did not come back.

Neither did they find her body.

Her family in Harare did not have a clue as to where she had gone.

In fact, they suspected foul play.

Some of her brothers thought that Mutereri had killed their sister and dumped her in a ditch somewhere and pretended she had disappeared.

Mutereri pleaded his innocence.

Now he had three kids under six to look after.

As he didn't have a maid, he took three months leave from work to get himself organized.

As maids in Harare were a bit out of his budget, Mutereri had to look for one from the countryside.

The first maid quit after two weeks.

She said the work load was too heavy for her. She could not cope.

The second maid ran away after a month.

She did not inform Mutereri in advance.

Just eloped leaving the children with a neighbour.

The third maid did not last a day.

She said 3 young children under the age of six were just not her cup of tea and bolted.

Mutereri found the kids all by themselves in the lounge.

Mutereri wept like a baby.

He was at his wits' end as to what to do.

He could not throw away the children

He could not bolt on the children

He could not hand over the children to someone else to look after.

His in-laws were already on his case as it was and were watching him like a hawk.

So, he single handedly looked after the three children, taking them to nursery during the day and fetching them by late afternoon after his shift at school was over.

Gone was his freedom

Gone was his free time

Gone was his Marjory.

Soon, word got out that his third wife had been the one who jilted him!

Those whom he had wronged just looked at him and shook their heads, possibly thinking 'Toko waro! - serves him right!'

The elder children he had ditched went on with their lives without him

Now he had to change nappies, prepare food for his three young children, bathe them, read them bed time stories, help them with their homework.

Life was far from easy.

10 years later, Mutereri got news through the grapevine that Marjory had been living and working in Brazil all this time.

'BRAZIL ?!!'

Mutereri could hardly believe it!!

Word has it that a white family had contracted her to work for them as a maid.

Mutereri wept.

With time, the kids grew up, got married and had children of their own.

Another 10 years passed.

Mutereri then met and married this woman in Mhondoro who was obese, dark in complexion, simple in thought and deed, no formal education to talk of, 20 years his Junior, with rather questionable morals.

Everyone in the family called her 'Mbuya Dhafu'

By this time, Mutereri was in his seventies.

He fathered five children with this woman, although many family members were sceptical about him being the real father.

The names of the children were: Maribho; Amon; Blair; A ....

Can't remember the other names!!

Mukai, Arise!

Chapter 11 - The Reunion

The Reunion.

'Let us not look back in anger nor forward in fear

but around us in awareness' ~Leland Val Van De Wall

'Let the dead bury the dead'

Meaning stop looking back in your life and worrying about things which have already occurred and which you can no longer alter.

Project into the future and do not be labour over things which had already past.

It was with this thought in mind that Mukai Mukundu Chapfumbu and her family decided to hold a get together party, for the first time ever.

Afterall, life is meant to be celebrated, right?

December 1983

Christmas, Boxing Day and Reunion all woven into one!

Wow!

What an occasion to remember!!

Family and friends, far and wide came to grace this great occasion.

Family from Mukai 's father's side of the family, came Family from Mukai's mother's side of the family came

Family from Laurentia 's side of the family, came.

Friends from yesteryear; friends recently acquired; friends intending to be acquired ... all came.

Church mates flocked to this event.

The Catholic community belonging to Edias and Laurentia, came.

The Dutch community belonging to Mukai Mukumbu Chapfumbu, came.

Colleagues from Edias' work place came.

Colleagues from Laurentia's work place came.

All roads led to No. 57A Umsungwe Block, Sangari Farm, Gweru!

You would see cars of different types, shapes, sizes, models slowing down, indicate to the right, and slowly drive through the already open gate.

"Welcome! Welcome!"

Mukai Mukundu Chapfumbu and her daughter-in-law, Laurentia Eunah, could be seen welcoming their guests to their 'humble' aboard.

'Humble' my foot!в

Even Mutereri Mutubuki aka Fedest Sapeta was invited!

And he came !!

Looking handsome and distinguished, Mutereri came dressed in his best.

My, and was he beaming from ear to ear!

Afterall, this was a mighty auspicious occasion!!

He was going to reunite with all his clan.

Even the children he had with Fadzai were invited and they came.

Even the children he had with Marjory had been invited and they came.

Amon came.

Vandudzai came.

Unfortunately, Mukai's beloved step-brother, Kota, could not come because he had died during the liberation struggle.

Otherwise had he been alive, he sure would have not missed this great event on the social calendar of The Mutubuki family.

However, Mukai was sure that her brother was there with her in spirit.

Any celebration wouldn't be complete without FOOD, now, would it?!!

This get together was no different.

Two huge heifers were specially selected from Mukai's 100 herd of cattle.

These two heifers were to be slaughtered for this occasion.

An abattoir in Gweru was assigned the awesome task of slaughtering, cutting, preparing and packing the beef.

A dozen goats lost their lives to grace this occasion with their meat!

And the number of chickens ... Mukai estimated that they were in the triple digits of 100 plus.

Waingonzwa 'kwekwerere .... kwekwerere .. kwekwerere ... kwekwerere ... dziri huku dzaibatwa muchirugu!!

Lots of commotion in the chicken run as they were being grabbed for the slaughter.

Poor chickens!!

What about different varieties of fish ... bream or tilapia, mackerel, sardines, salmon, white fish ... you name it, it was available.

Kuzoti rice, different varieties of cereals and forms of starch dishes like sorghum, millet, rapoko, mapfunde, wheat ...

Let us not forget the different varieties of vegetables to prepare salads and soup dishes with ...

Breakfast items like tea, coffee, milk, bread, margarine, butter, eggs, freshly baked scones ...

During those three days, people ate; people danced; people sang; people listened to music; people laughed, people listened to stories ...

BBQ!

Beef, Chicken, Goat meat, corn were the order of the day.

Fires and hot ash could be seen in numerous BBQ stands scattered around the BBQ area.

Vazukuru nevakuwasha - nephews and sons-in-law were the ones tasked with this prestigious role.

You would see a perfect caricature of division of labour.

Some of the nephews and sons-in-law could be seen cutting firewood ... others preparing the fire in the BBQ stands ... others preparing the meat for BBQ.

Those tasked with distribution of the actual finished product could be seen collecting the paper plates and trays they were going to serve in.

It was a lovely sight to behold.

Soon enough, the aroma emanating from yonder was so tantalising, all the youngsters gravitated towards the area hoping for a piece or two of the delicious braai.

Those who drank, drank till they dropped.

Everyone was happy.

It was like one big family ... which of course, they were.

Mukai let bygones be bygones .

Mutereri let bygones be bygones.

All the children let bygones be bygones.

Forgiveness, healing, starting over ... was the overall meal dished out over these three days.

A lot of bonding took place.

A lot of introductions were made.

"Hoo ... saka ndiye Mukai wacho wembiri uyu ...?!"

Referring to Mukai 's eldest granddaughter

You see, when Mukai Henrieta was born, as is typical of African Shona culture, the parents were no longer addressed by their names.

Instead, they are addressed by their eldest child's name.

New parents assumed a new identity, if you will.

Its like an Actor or Author who takes on a new identity; a new name; a pseudonym.

It's a celebration of a new life, a new lifestyle, a new form of responsibility.

Parenthood is one taking on a new character.

In this case,

Edias became known as 'Baba vaMukai'

Laurentia became known as 'Mai vaMukai'

Mukai Mukumbu Chapfumbu became known as 'Mbuya vaMukai'

Coban Chambiwa - Laurentia 's youngest brother who stayed with them became known as 'Sekuru vaMukai' ...

It was crazy!

"Ohh ... so this is Chandirekera Sarah ...?!

I am so happy to meet you ..."

"Gamuchirai, come say hello to your aunt, Mbuya Mai Pepukai ...!"

"Fungai ... have you said 'Good morning' to your grandfather?!"

"Mukai bring the dish and some water for your grandfather to wash his hands in !"

"Tete Maema ... huyai kuno!"

"Tete Grace, mamuka sei?"

"Shepherd, hauna kundikwazisa nhasi. Hindava?!"

"Ini handina kudya kana chinhu kubva chimukiro ..!!" Seretse complained looking very distraught

"Alright, Abamunini.

Hold on.

I will bring you some food"

Mukai Henrieta replied and rushed off

"Uri bhoo here muzukuru?!"

Murimo Chambiwa, Laurentia's step-brother asked as he placed young Fungai on his lap.

"Sisi, chimbouyai kuno?"

Laurentia addressed her eldest sister, Shirley

"Hapana anondida pamusha pano !!"

Shirley sulked

"What can I do to be of service?!"

Perpetua Pedzisa Karimazondo, Laurentia's cousin, asked

Throughout all these festivities, something interesting was brewing in the air ...

Everyone had been busy with everyone else to notice what was beginning to germinate right under their noses ...

Edias was the one who noticed it first.

They say kids miss nothing that their parents get up to.

Edias was no different!

He noticed it, kwaakutsonya his wife , saying

"Hona ... !! "

Using his mouth to direct her attention towards his intended subject, in this case, it was plural ... subjects !!

Laurentia was puzzled by the look in her husband's eyes and wondered what or who he was referring to.

She followed his gaze.

Lo behold, a sight she never thought she would ever behold in her lifetime was staring her right in front of her ...

Mukai Mukundu Chapfumbu was strolling hand in hand with Fedest Sapeta!!

The overall picture they created ... they looked like young lovers!!

They were a distance from the others, but the naked eye could make out who they were.

They were engrossed in deep conversation.

Laurentia opened her mouth, totally speechless and looked back at her husband.

The two just looked at each other, smiled, winked at each other and shook their heads.

Christmas came, followed by Boxing Day, then the next day.

What was meant as three days of celebration, stretched to one week.

Then as the New Year of 1984 settled in, one by one, people started to reluctantly take their leave.

Unfortunately, they needed to get back to their workplaces ... kids needed to get back to school ... routines needed to be reestablished.

Some returned to Harare, others to Masvingo; some dissipated into Gweru.

A large group returned to Gutu ... Mutare ... Rusape ... Bulawayo ... Chivhu ...

The noise and excitement that had been the hallmark at No. 57A Umsungwe Block in the last week settled down into a comfortable silence as the two 'love birds' strolled along the road, deep in conversation.

Mukai Mukundu Chapfumbu and Fedest Sapeta were rekindling where they had left off about 35 years ago.

They had a lot to catch up on.

So much had happened.

So much needed to be said.

All the kids were now grown and had kids of their own. They were scattered all over the country.

When everyone else had gone, it was just the two of them left at No. 57A Umsungwe Block ... with the servants, of course.

Would it work this time?

Edias and Laurentia wondered

Would his parents' relationship work this time? Edias wondered

How would he feel about it, not that it was his decision to make.

His parents' affair was none of his business.

He was not going to interfere.

Forgiveness.

What does forgiveness really mean in a relationship between two people?

Does it mean when you forgive someone, you automatically trust them again?

Whereas forgiveness is given freely and willingly, trust has to be earned.

It can't be demanded.

Neither can it be forced.

So, when a relationship breaks down the first time, is it wise to try again years later and make it work?

What would have changed during that time?

Is it possible to overlook what had transpired in the past and take the relationship to another level?

Can a person really change?

Should they change?

Or just remain who they are and in the process, look for someone who resonates with who they are?

Does anyone have a right to expect the other person to change; or even go to the extent of demanding that they change?

Manipulation and deception.

Can a relationship work when one party has ulterior motives - a hidden agenda?

Can a relationship work if the other is entering into the relationship for the sole reason as to what they think they can get out of the other person; not necessarily for love per se?

Love and compatibility.

Does it mean if we love someone, we can be compatible with them?

Isn't it possible to love someone but realize that the two simply cannot live with each other.

When a deep hurt or betrayal has been committed by one partner in the relationship, is it possible to forget and pick up where you left off?

Forgiving in advance.

There is talk of forgiving in advance; that is forgive your partner before he or she actually commits the betrayal because no one is immune to sin, including yourself.

Those are the million dollar questions each of us have to face at some point in our lives.

Well, the bottom line is this.

In Mukai Mukumbu Chapfumbu's case, she could not make her relationship with Mutereri Mutubuki work between 1946 and 1948; neither could she make it work with Fedest Sapeta, 35 years later, in 1984.

Three months after these two had rekindled their relationship, once again they were involved in a huge row and broke up.

It is said the reason for the row and subsequent break up was that Mutereri had suggested that he move in permanently in No. 57A Umsungwe Block.

Mukai Mukundu Chapfumbu had regarded this as Mutereri's way of 'worming' his way into Edias ' life and take over the farm.

No. 57A Umsungwe Block was Edias' property.

Mukai Mukumbu Chapfumbu was living under the care of his son and daughter - in - law.

She felt that had Mutereri's intentions been genuine, and he really wanted to be with HER; then he should have asked her to come live with him in HIS own home in Mhondoro, instead of suggesting he move in with her at her son's place.

Of course, Fedest Sapeta denied the allegations and said she was overreacting.

It is said after this row, Mukai threw Fedest Sapeta out.

That was that.

Edias had to drive to No. 57A Umsungwe Block to fetch his father in the middle of the night.

Mukai had been livid when she called him and demanded he come pick up his father and send him on the first bus back to Mhondoro where he was staying.

A day later, Mutereri was on that first bus ride back to his home.

That was that, sadza repaBoarding.

Mukai, Arise!

Chapter 12 - Return to normalcy, or is it?

After Mutereri left, Mukai Mukumbu Chapfumbu's life returned to normal.

Her life revolved around her life at the farm at No. 57A Umsungwe Block; her son, her daughter-in-law, her granddaughters and her church mates.

To empower her granddaughters and welcome them into this world, Mukai had a habit of opening Bank Accounts for each granddaughter after it was born.

She opened the Accounts with POSB.

The money would accumulate interest.

By the time each granddaughter turned 7, they could withdraw whatever cash they required.

Talk about economic empowerment and shrewd business sense!!

And Talk about a perfect illustration of how family sticks, defends and protects one other against bullies ...

Picture this!!

Mukai Mukundu Chapfumbu's youngest granddaughter, Ropafadzo, affectionately known as Ropo, used to be bullied at school by this boy called John Huruva.

She, along with her two elder sisters, Fungai and Tinotenda used to attend the same school, Cecil John Rhodes in Gweru.

The school was a bus ride away from home.

Ropafadzo was in Grade 1 or Grade 2 - thereabouts.

Big sister, Tinotenda, Mukai Mukundu Chapfumbu's 5th granddaughter got wind of the bullying one day when Ropafadzo was now crying in the bus on their way back home after school.

Let me quote Tinotenda verbatim as she related the event in her own words to Ropafadzo ... "Was it not John Huruva ... he used to beat you up.

I think you were in Grade 1 or 2 and that made me soooooo upset and angry cause you would cry at home time.

I decided to deal with him.

He was even a thief.

Bara raakarova pandakamudzingirira pa home time takamirira bhazi ...

I caught him ndikamupa chibhakera heyi; hameno kuti akatsukunyuka sei from my hand akatiza ncmmmmmmm.

Haaana kuzorova Ropo again ."

KKK...

Overall translation!!

Big sister Tinotenda beat up the bully so thoroughly he never beat nor bullied Ropo ever again!!

"Now, that's how you deal with bullies!!" Big sister Fungai remarked!!

KKK ...

Mutereri returned to his present wife, Mbuya Dhafu in Mhondoro and their five children.

Life returned to normal.

He was now retired and spent all his time at home.

There were times he used to visit his eldest son, Edias at his home, now at No. 14 Laverton Estate, Claremont Road, Shurugwi Road in Daylesford, Gweru.

A few months after The Reunion in 1984, Edias bought the property next door to No.13

The previous owner, a white couple by the name of O'Connor were relocating to Harare to be with their grown up children.

No. 14 was a beautiful, well maintained place.

It was definitely a step up from No. 13

The O'Connors had put their blood and sweat into this place.

It was a marvel ... like a place you only see in magazines.

5 hectares of arable, rich, fertile land.

Well kept !

Well maintained !

Lawn and rose bushes, perfectly manicured !

A real feast for the eyes.

For starters, The O'Connors boasted well bred and glitzy horses which could be seen galloping and grazing in one of the paddocks.

Every morning, the stable hand could be gleaned at the stables busy brushing the horses' hide till it shown.

The O'Connors also grew roses for export.

The flowers had the most beautiful shape, stunning velvety texture and at close range, they exuded the most exquisite fragrance.

The house itself boasted a 3 bedroom brick under tile roof.

The roof tiles were painted black.

The external walls were white washed.

The way into the house was through a Single Leaf Stable Door that led one directly into the scullery, then into the kitchen that had the most breathtaking kitchen cupboards - brown in colour.

Laurentia's favourite colour.

Directly infront, a wooden Sliding Door led to the Laundry Room.

The other Single Leaf Door to the left led directly into a TV Room cum Dining Room.

A beautiful fireplace could be glimpsed to the right.

A well stocked bar, demarcated the TV Room from the Dining Room.

Elegant black chandeliers draped from the white ceiling.

A hue of colours could be gleaned on the small chapel type windows to the left.

The colour scheme was white - matt finish.

A square arch led directly into a spacious lounge.

The colour scheme in this room was sky blue - matt finish.

The same type of fireplace could be glimpsed to the left.

And the same type of black chandeliers dangled from the white ceiling .

An impressive collection of books adorned the shelves of a cabinet to the right.

A French window, burglar barred, abutted the full breadth of one wall directly infront.

French Double Leaf Doors opened directly onto a lovely veranda that had a stone floor.

Back inside the house, a corridor led to a nook that was also serviced by a door.

This nook was used as a study area by his daughters.

It was also used as a telephone booth.

The colour scheme here was purple - matt finish.

Really appealing to the eye.

Further along the corridor took you to the three bedrooms and a bathroom with a separate wc.

The main bedroom was ensuite.

The whole house, except the bathrooms, kitchen, scullery and laundry room had parquet flooring.

For added security, all the windows had burglar bars.

A garage cum greenhouse was located at the front of the yard.

A spacious tool room abutted this garage.

Veering off to the right from the gate, took one along a corridor in the form of a neatly trimmed hedge.

A few paces along, you would arrive at a Workers Quarters.

It was self contained with two separate rooms, a cooking area and a bathroom.

In their garden, The O'connors grew strawberries.

In the orchard, they had lemon trees that produced the juiciest lemons one has ever tasted.

Oranges, Paw paws, pears, apples, peaches were plentiful.

Mutereri used to just rest at his son's new place silently reflecting - his mind far away - totally oblivious of his six granddaughters playing around him, and from time to time trying to get his attention by tugging at his sleeve and plead "Grandpa ... please tell us a story ..."

All granddaughters would look expectantly at him.

And he would snap "Go away!!

Go play somewhere!

Don't you have homework to finish ... books to read ... or television to watch!!" With that he would turn around and go back to his brooding.

The grand kids would scuttle away and play by themselves.

Little did he realise that he had just missed that one in a million chance to bond with his grandchildren.

The tragedy is that the grandchildren never developed a relationship with him.

Once again, like he did with his son, he missed that opportunity to get to know and bond with his granddaughters.

Pity.

Sad.

Tragic.

A life full of regrets can blind one to the reality of love that is staring at one in the face.

Mutereri missed the love that had been staring at him in the six faces of his young granddaughters.

Years passed.

No remarkable drama until one fateful day...

The year was now 1987 ...

A most unexpected news reached the ears of Mutereri ...

Apparently, Marjory was coming back!!

She was scheduled to land at Harare International Airport from Brazil later that week on a Friday.

Maema, who was living and working in Harare had telephoned him to inform him of this news He was in Mhondoro.

"What?!"

He had exclaimed

"Yes, Baba, Mamma is coming back.

Grace, Shepherd and our kids are going to wait for her at the airport."

"Really?"

Mutereri remarked, cringing at the news.

"And where will she be staying?" He asked

"She will rotate.

We will take turns to stay with her.

First, it will be me who will stay with her for a few months; then Shepherd and his wife, Mai Susan.

.

Lastly, Grace will take her in.

The process will repeat itself after that."

The news that Marjory, popularly known as 'Mbuya Brazil' was coming home from South America after a 30 year absence travelled throughout the country so fast, the way a bee travels from one plant to another in search of nectar.

Everyone in the family was amazed and those who hadn't met her in person; but had heard of her fame, looked forward to meeting her.

Even Mukai Mukundu Chapfumbu's granddaughters looked forward to meeting this 'heroine' in the family who had finally managed to cut the great Mutereri Mutubuki aka Fedest Sapeta to size!!

Her arrival was also very fortuitous for her youngest daughter, Kwaedza Grace, had recently completed her studies as a teacher at Gweru Teacher's College.

Her graduation ceremony was due shortly and her mother, Mbuya Brazil, was expected to attend.

Standards!!

Whoever said a little competition doesn't come in handy at times!

Having gotten wind that one of her 'rivals' was coming to town, Mukai Mukundu Chapfumbu had dug deep into her wardrobe and brought out one of her best outfits to wear to Kwaedza Grace's function.

The day of her graduation arrived.

Mukai , Edias, Laurentia and their six girls dressed in their best, made their way to Gweru Teacher's College.

Kwaedza Grace looked distinguished and learned clad in her graduation gown!

Oh what a moment!!

The one thing Mukai Mukumbu Chapfumbu loved and admired most about the culture in

Zimbabwe is the way the people made time to celebrate excellence and academic achievement!! It made the whole toil, blood and sweat of the previous three, four, seven years worth it.

During graduation ceremonies, you'd find family members, all dressed in beautiful outfits, making their way to the College or University holding the function.

The graduates would be dressed in their absolute best with the graduation gowns draped over their newly purchased suits and caps in one hand.

The ululation, the joy and the congratulations the graduant received was like no other!!

It was a proud moment, indeed !!

At the venue, the graduates would be seated infront in one area, arranged by Faculty.

The family members, friends and colleagues would occupy the seats at the back, anxiously waiting for the occasion to begin.

Whenever the name of their graduand was called out, the graduate would stand up, walk smartly and proudly to the front to be capped by The Chancellor.

In the back drop, mukurumbira - celebrations - would be in hot pursuit - the mother ... the sister ... the niece ... the guardian ... would be speeding at 120km/hr towards their graduand ululating and exclaiming words of praise going as far back as the ancestral lineage ....

"Mwana wangu iyeye!!

Haadyi chimwe chinhu!!

Maita Mukanya Soko, Vhudzijena !!

Zvirambe zvakadaro!!

Hekani waro!! Nhasi ndezveduwo!!"

Translation - literal!

"That's my baby!

He/She doesn't eat anything else !

Thank you my baby of the Soko totem !

May you continue to shine!

Wow!

Today is our day!"

It was a beautiful, moving and touching moment to witness.

To see and witness such shear joy; sheer happiness; celebration at it's best!

Wow!

For the aspiring graduands, say those who were still studying at school - it was a very motivating moment indeed.

The same kind of celebration lay in store for Kwaedza Grace.

When her name was called, The Mutubuki clan could be seen running towards their family member, ululating, jumping for joy, praising all the wonderful forces of this universe.

Hugs and hugs were everywhere!!

Among the celebrants was this 60 plus lady ... yes, lady ... dressed in a blood red three piece suit, six inch high heels, pulling stockings, hair styled into beautiful curls, clutching a leather handbag.

She was hugging and congratulating Kwaedza Grace going "Congratulations my daughter!!

You did us proud!"

That is when Mukai Mukundu Chapfumbu and her family had the their first glimpse of the famous Marjory!!

Verbal descriptions of her hadn't exaggerated!

In fact, they had sold her short!

Marjory WAS BEAUTIFUL!!

She was light in complexion ... to the side of white.

She stood at a stunning 6 foot 8 inches

She had a lovely personality and laughed easily. She was very friendly

In short, she was a breath of fresh air.

"Wow!"

The six granddaughters uttered in unison the first time they laid their eyes on her.

Even Edias and Laurentia looked impressed!!

They were smiling from ear to ear.

Even Mukai Mukundu Chapfumbu was impressed!!

Wow!

Now everyone knew what Fedest Sapeta had seen in this roaring beauty.

If her inner character matched her physical looks, then she would be an angel.

But as the Shona say

'Mukadzi mutsvuku, mudodo; kana akasaba, anoroya!'

Translation!

'Still waters run deep!' Time would prove this point.

Read on!

A year later, health challenges sprang up in the family.

Mutereri developed cataract initially in one eye.

Edias tried to take him to see a specialist in Harare and have the cataract surgically removed, but he refused.

He said he was afraid that if he was put under anaesthetic, he would not wake up.

Two years later, he developed cataract in the other eye.

He was now completely blind.

Mbuya Dhafu used to call Edias and complain about Mutereri.

She said he was difficult to live with; was petulant and careless with his tongue.

Edias did not know how to respond to this.

He would only listen.

Shortly thereafter, accusations between husband and wife wormed their way to the surface.

Mutereri alleged that his wife had a habit of 'disappearing' for many hours at a time; and he would not know where she had been.

When he confronted her about it, she would be rude to him.

In protest to this bad behaviour, one of his daughters took him in her care in Harare.

Citing that Mbuya Dhafu was not competent enough to look after him, Maema took over the responsibility of looking after her father.

She stayed with him for a few years.

Then tragedy struck

The year was 1999, Mutereri Sapeta passed on.

This was not before he had made amends with his eldest granddaughter, Mukai Henrieta.

In the preceding year before he died, whenever Mukai Henrieta called her father, Edias, he would end his conversation with the words "Your grandfather is always asking after you.

Please go to Harare and see him"

Mukai Henrieta would always reply

"Yes, Dad"

But she never did

This pattern of conversation continued for close to a year, until one day it finally dawned on Mukai Henrieta that in fact her father was actually serious!

Her grandfather REALLY wanted her to visit and see him!!

The thing is, over the years, Mukai Henrieta had never bonded with her grandfather.

To her, he existed physically, yes.

If she was asked to point and identify who her grandfather was, she could point towards him.

But emotionally, if she was asked to find and locate her grandfather in one of the chambers of her heart, she could not, for he had never occupied a place in it in the first place.

To Mukai Henrieta, it was just one of those things.

So, when her father had been referring to his father's wish, it had not clicked immediately into her subconscious mind that, indeed, her grandfather truly wanted to see her.

So, one fine day she made her way to Harare to see her grandfather.

She had called in advance.

When she arrived, her grandfather was waiting by the gate.

Her aunt Maema said he had been waiting like this for close to an hour.

Any attempt at making him go inside the house was marked with the worst retort imaginable.

So, they had let him be.

When Mukai Henrieta finally made her appearance - handikufara ikoko!!

Mutereri was so overjoyed.

He was smiling, laughing, joking ... TELLING STORIES!!

It was incredible!!

Her grandfather who had always been cool towards her was a changed man!!

He was chatty.

He was exciting to be around.

He was fun to hang around with!

Now, THIS was the grandfather she had always yearned for!!

THIS was how grandfathers were supposed to be with their grandchildren.

Present.

Emotionally available.

Chatty.

Supportive.

Engaging.

Motivational.

Life was good!!

They had spoken for hours the rest of that afternoon that stretched far into the night.

Her aunt Maema commented that of all the years she had known her father, she had never seen him this happy.

Mukai Henrieta had finally taken her leave way past midnight, albeit reluctantly.

Mutereri Mutubuki aka Fedest Sapeta breathed his last six months later.

He was close to 80.

Mutereri Mutubuki may not have been able to make amends directly with his wife, Mukai Mukundu Chapfumbu Mutubuki, but he sure made amends with her, vicariously, through THEIR eldest granddaughter, Mukai Henrieta Mutubuki.

The proceedings and events of that day at Maema's household point to this fact.

And its significant that this healing had to take place in the home of the daughter he loved and cherished so much.

It is a fact.

Mutereri loved, adored, admired and worshipped the ground his daughter, Maema, walked on.

If one looks back, in hindsight, one notices that in fact, Mutereri had been trying to make amends with his eldest son, Edias, through the namesake and I believe he succeeded.

He requested Edias and Laurentia to name his granddaughters after four powerful, influential women he cared the most about:

Mukai Henrieta in February of 1972

Chandirekera Sarah in May of 1973

Gamuchirai in February of 1976

Fungai in June of 1981

You see, all these years he had been trying to make amends and as I have already mentioned above, I believe he succeeded.

I am 100% sure that when Mutereri Mutubuki aka Fedest Sapeta passed on, he passed away a relaxed person, having made peace with all the ghosts of the past. May his soul rest in peace

Mukai, Arise!

Chapter 13 - Bereavement

Mukai Henrieta noticed that her grandmother, Mukai Mukundu Chapfumbu, had lost her will to live after she heard the news of Mutereri's passing.

She remembers her grandmother lamenting in a mournful way "Mutereri waenda!! - meaning Mutereri is gone!"

Her voice had shook with emotion.

She had not shed a tear ... not in Mukai Henrieta's presence anyway, but she had looked sad ... very sad indeed.

Mukai Henrieta felt her pain, her sadness, her loss.

From then on, Mukai Mukundu Chapfumbu walked about aimlessly without any interest in her surroundings.

It was like nothing interested her anymore.

Is it possible that, that young woman of 24 never gave up hope of a reconciliation between herself and her beloved?

Is it possible that in her heart of hearts, Mukai Mukundu Chapfumbu never stopped loving Mutereri inspite of everything that had transpired between them?

Is it possible that Mukai Mukundu Chapfumbu, when all was said and done, she saw things more clearly ... that in relationships, what matters is not about being right, but about just trying as much as possible to live in love and harmony with the one you are with.

So what if you are right and he is wrong ?

So what if so and so wronged you?

So what if the one you are with thinks differently from you ? Is different wrong or just that ... different.

A man and a woman, shouldn't they COMPLEMENT each other, rather than COMPETE with each other?

Well, I guess, a woman has a right to her secrets, secrets that torment her heart.

Or is it possible that age, as well, had taken its toll?

Afterall, Mukai Mukundu Chapfumbu was more nearing 80.

Whatever the actual reason, Mukai Mukundu Chapfumbu slowly, but surely retreated into herself.

She no longer spoke.

She rarely smiled.

She was now prone to going off on her own and spending long periods of time in solitude.

I guess that's what happens when someone has a broken heart.

Possibly this time, Mukai Mukundu Chapfumbu was really mourning the loss of a man she had ironically lost more than five decades previously.

Maybe that time in 1948 when Mutereri left, Mukai Mukundu Chapfumbu did not have the luxury to sit and wallow in her sadness.

She had a baby to think of.

So, maybe she had let adrenaline propel her forward doing what needed to be done to provide for her son.

Now, 50 plus years later she had to face head on, the face of grief, the face of loss and the harsh and cruel reality of death!!

Abandonment number five had reared its ugly presence yet again, now in the form of the death of the only man she ever possibly truly loved, Mutereri Mutubuki aka Fedest Sapeta.

What was she going to do now?

Her true North was gone!

She was now like a compass without proper coordinates, just flaying about in the wind like a seashore without a lighthouse; a ship without a sail.

2000; 2001; 2003 great grandchildren were now being added into the mix.

The family was growing.

Earlier in 1997, December 27th, Mukai Mukundu Chapfumbu's eldest great granddaughter, Angela Runyararo Kumirai, had been the latest addition into the family.

29th May 2001, her second great grandson had followed. His name, Michael Panashe Kumirai.

Mukai Henrieta is the mother to these two awesome great grandchildren.

24th January 2003 her third great grandson, Ayanda Sean Makuyana was born.

Coincidentally, this handsome, unusually tall great - grandson shares a birthday with his grandfather, Edias !

How is that for providence ??!!

Incidentally, Mukai Henrieta shares the exact birth date with her aunt, Kwaedza Grace - 25th February!!

Imagine!!

In 2005, Andile Nhlanhla Makuyana was born.

He is such an adorable boy; sweet; thoughtful; centred; happy.

Chandirekera Sarah is the mother to these two great grandchildren.

March 2005, Mukai Mukundu Chapfumbu passed away peacefully in her sleep at No. 14 Laverton Estate, Claremont Road, Shurugwi Road, Gweru.

Her granddaughter, Fungai, found her.

She had not been breathing.

A GIANT HAD FALLEN!!

Mukai Mukundu Chapfumbu, a true woman of substance was no more.

A girl, a daughter, a granddaughter, a lover, a wife, a mother, a mother-in-law, a grandmother, a great-grandmother, a sister, a friend, a helper, a teacher.

Generous to a fault.

Powerful beyond measure.

Principled even to the detriment of some of her most prized and treasured relationships.

Astute.

Confident.

Poised.

Knew her mind and lived by her principles.

Strong.

Courageous.

Victorious.

Lived her life to the fullest.

Perfect illustration and role model of what it means to be a woman in a society dominated by men.

Perfect illustration and role model of what it takes to survive and go onto thrive in a society full of booby traps in terms of people's hidden agendas, malice, deception.

Perfect illustration and role model of what it takes to be true to yourself and live your life in accordance with how you see it.

A woman who stared truth in the face, rather than hide behind her finger or bury her head, ostrich - like, in the sand.

A woman who fought for herself, her son, her daughter-in-law, her granddaughters and her great-grandchildren.

A woman like no other.

Again, that March morning, two weeks after her passing, all roads led to No. 57A Umsungwe Block, not to party, but to pay their last respects to a great lady, a true champion, a true woman of substance.

Mukai Mukundu Chapfumbu Mutubuki !!

May her gracious soul rest in peace!!

Mukai, Arise!

Chapter 14 - Barika

Life continued after Mukai Mukundu Chapfumbu Mutubuki 's passing.

More great grandchildren were born and still are going to be born.

As I said before, barika rakaoma!!

Mukai Mukundu Chapfumbu Mutubuki 's story would not be complete if I do not touch on the effects of barika - the politics and dilemma that lies behind it ... the back biting ... the hypocrisy ... the heart ache ... the malice ... the deception ... the back biting ... the competition for resources ... the jealousy ... the manipulation ...

The tug of war that ensues can be a real pain for the children left behind.

The same was true for Edias and some of the children of Mutereri Mutubuki aka Fedest Sapeta.

A few years after Mukai Mukundu Chapfumbu Mutubuki's passing, Marjory filed a case in The High Court citing that she was the 'legitimate' and 'lawful' wife of the deceased, Fedest Mutubuki, meaning her three children, Maema, Shepherd and Kwaedza Grace were the ONLY 'legitimate' children of Fedest Sapeta.

Ironically, she was correct!!

'What?!'

You may be thinking.

Read on, I say!!

By this motion what Marjory was actually trying to say was that Edias, Seretse, Enesia, Nyasha Cleopas, Maribho et al were not legitimate children of Mutereri Mutubuki aka Fedest Sapeta.

She did this in order to lay claim on Mutereri's property in Mhondoro and wrestle out the current official wife, Mbuya Dhafu.

Marjory produced a Marriage Certificate with the name 'Fedest Mutubuki' written on it, as evidence to prove her point.

This motion had been filed secretly.

The audacity of a woman who had bolted on her three children when they were still babies and had stayed away without a word for 30 years, and now here she was laying claim to a man she had walked out on without a backward glance!

Luckily, Kwaedza Grace wouldn't be party to such a preposterous allegation and alerted her step-brother, Edias.

On the prescribed Court date, Edias accompanied by his wife, Laurentia and step-sister, Kwaedza Grace, step-brothers, Seretse and Nyasha Cleopas made their way to the court.

When they saw them walk in the courtroom, Marjory, Maema and Shepherd were said to have looked very shocked.

'How had Edias, Seretse and Nyasha Cleopas known about these proceedings AND why was Kwaedza Grace coming in with THEM?!!' look.

The presiding judge was a female.

When the judge had asked if there were any children who disagreed with the statement, Edias had stood up and objected and gone onto describe in detail, Mutereri Mutubuki aka Fedest Sapeta aka Fedest Mutubuki's lifestyle throughout the years.

As evidence he produced a certified copy of Mutereri Mutubuki's Class 3 motorbike License which had written on it the name Mutereri Mutubuki, NOT Fedest Sapeta or Fedest Mutubuki !!

As further evidence, Edias produced a certified copy of his father's ID which had a picture of him on it.

The name written there was Mutereri Mutubuki, NOT Fedest Sapeta or Fedest Mutubuki!!

Edias gave the High Court Judge all these certified copies of the deceased plus Title Deeds of his Mhondoro Stand and Store.

The name written there was Mutereri Mutubuki, NOT Fedest Sapeta or Fedest Mutubuki!!

No man under the name of Fedest Sapeta or Fedest Mutubuki owned any property.

Apparently Fedest Sapeta and or Fedest Mutubuki were just pseudonyms Mutereri Mutubuki used orally only and were not on any of his IDs.

Maema's ID had the name Sapeta as her maiden name.

In impeccable English, Edias also went onto describe in sordid detail how Marjory had walked out on her alleged 'husband' and three very young babies and stayed away without a word for 30 years in South America.

So, the Chapter 37 Marriage Certificate Marjory had been wielding as evidence in the High Court did not belong to the deceased, Mutereri Mutubuki.

The Marriage Certificate proved that she was indeed a married woman; to a Fedest Mutubuki; but this man did not exist ... had never existed!!

At least not on paper, anyway!!

Her marriage had been a fluke!!

There was no such man in Zimbabwe by the name of Fedest Mutubuki!!

He simply did not exist!!

Which also meant that Maema Sapeta, Shepherd Sapeta, Kwaedza Grace Sapeta, Seretse Sapeta, Enesia Sapeta, Cleopas Nyasha Sapeta, Maribho Sapeta et al had been fathered by a man who doesn't exist!!

THE ONLY LEGITIMATE CHILD OF MUTERERI MUTUBUKI WAS EDIAS HENRY KANAMADERO MUTUBUKI, the son he had had with MUKAI MUKUNDU CHAPFUMBU MUTUBUKI !!!

How do you like that for a twist?!!

The conman had struck again!!

This time even from the grave!!

10: 0 !!

The case was dismissed.

A short while later, outside, after the Court proceedings, Edias, Laurentia, Kwaedza Grace, Seretse and Nyasha Cleopas burst out laughing!!

Marjory, Maema and Shepherd had stormed out of the courtroom, earlier, panting and furious.

Their plan had fallen flat in their faces.

'Mukadzi mutsvuku, mudodo, akasaba, anoroya!'

Mukai, Arise!

Chapter 15 - The Legacy

The Legacy

The legacy of Mukai Mukundu Chapfumbu Mutubuki lives on.

It lives on in her son, Dr. Edias Henry Kanamadero Mutubuki and the legacy he co-created with his beloved, devoted, hard working, prayerful wife, Laurentia Eunah Chambiwa Mutubuki.

She was not only a loving and caring wife, but a loving, caring mother, teacher, daughter-in-law, sister, aunt, grandmother.

Mukai Mukundu Chapfumbu Mutubuki's daughter-in-law, Laurentia Eunah left a great legacy indeed in that she and Edias formed a Trust known as The Mutubuki Trust, constituting their four properties:

13 Laverton Estate, Plot, 5 hectares

14 Laverton Estate, Plot, 5 hectares

57A umsungwe Block, Farm, 400 hectares

200 A Fleming, Plot, 0.25 hectares

Their six children are trustees of the Trust, excluding their spouses as they do not possess the unique blood of Mukai Mukundu Chapfumbu Mutubuki.

And the Trust built a beautiful Secondary Boarding School at their stand sitaute at 13 Laverton Estate.

It is named Laura House Academy.

The Trust also built a Biomedical Institution and Wildlife Management College named Laura House College, registered under the Ministries of Higher Education and of Health and Childcare.

Again all roads lead to 57A Umsungwe Block and 13 Laverton Estate; this time to celebrate, immortalise and fortify Mukai Mukundu Chapfumbu Mutubuki 's excellence in the field of Education.

What a great Teacher she was - both in a Class in the school that she taught for more than 30 years and in the Class called 'Life'.

The Trust is legacy of Mukai Mukundu Chapfumbu Mutubuki, Edias Henry Kanamadero Mutubuki and Laurentia Eunah Chambiwa Mutubuki.

Mukai Mukundu Chapfumbu Mutubuki's legacy lives on in her SIX granddaughters scattered throughout the world.

The genes of education Mukai had passed on can be seen in the academic achievement her granddaughters and great-grandchildren went onto produce.

Mukai Henrieta in Dubai, United Arab Emirates.

She holds a Bachelor's degree - BSc Quantity Surveying with the University of KwaZulu - Natal in Durban, South Africa.

She is a Chartered Quantity Surveyor by profession - having been one of the two Quantity Surveyors in the whole country that year in May 2000 who sat and passed their Test of Professional Competence (TPC).

The other Quantity Surveyor who passed that year was Justin Majakwara in Harare.

Mukai Henrieta passed this extremely challenging exam after only one sitting - two years after graduation.

Mukai Henrieta also holds a Masters in Business Administration (MBA) which she obtained through National University of Science and Technology in Bulawayo whilst she was both Chairman of Department and Lecturer in a Department she chartered between September 2000 and September 2004.

Chandirekera Sarah in Harare, Zimbabwe

She holds a Bachelor of Commerce (Accounting) with University of Botswana.

She has an MSc in Accounting and Finance with the University of Birmingham, UK.

She is a Renewable Energy Consultant with in-depth knowledge of Renewable Energy Markets as well as special expertise in designing and developing Financing, Business and Economic Strategies and Models for ensuring Sustainability of decentralised energy delivery to isolated and Rural Communities.

Gamuchirai in London, England, UK

She holds a Bachelor's Degree in Civil Engineering with the University of Zimbabwe.

She also holds a Masters degree with a university in the UK.

Fungai in Saskatoon, Canada.

She holds a Bachelor's Degree in Quantity Surveying that she completed with National University of Science and Technology in Bulawayo, Zimbabwe.

She also holds a Master of Science in Project Management with Robert Gordon University in Aberdeen Scotland.

Tinotenda in Aberdeen, Scotland.

She holds a Bachelor's degree in Journalism and Media Studies which she completed with National University of Science and Technology in Bulawayo, Zimbabwe.

Tinotenda also completed a Graduate Diploma in Law with Nottingham University.

She is due to commence her Masters programme with the same university in the same field shortly.

Ropafadzo in Harare, Zimbabwe.

She holds a Bachelor's Degree in Business Administration that she completed with Solusi University in Solusi, Zimbabwe.

Mukai Mukundu Chapfumbu Mutubuki's legacy lives on in her TEN great grandchildren and counting ...

Angela Runyararo Kumirai who is now studying at Pennsylvania University in the United States of America.

She is Double Majoring in:

Bachelor of Arts in Chemistry and

Bachelor of Arts in Health and Societies with a concentration in Healthcare Markets and Finance.

She is due to graduate shortly.

Michael Panashe Kumirai who is now completing his A'Levels at Fletcher High School, Gweru, Zimbabwe.

He lives with his beloved grandfather, Edias Henry Kanamadero Mutubuki - a great man indeed.

Laurentia Eunah Chambiwa Mutubuki passed on on 19th May 2017.

She was the great matriarch who raised her two fantastic, powerful, intelligent, driven, phenomenally successful grandchildren; Angela Runyararo Kumirai and Michael Panashe Kumirai.

Thank you Mum!!

I love you !!

May your soul rest in peace.

Ayanda Sean and Andile Nhlanhla Makuyana living with their parents, Chandirekera Sarah and Nhlanhla Makuyana and studying in Harare, Zimbabwe.

Anashe, Anotidaishe and Anesu Edias Marowa living with their parents, Fungai and Noel Marowa, and studying abroad in Saskatoon, Canada.

Sapphire and Zayn Okere living with their parents Tinotenda and Alozie Okere, and studying abroad in Aberdeen, Scotland.

Tayana Eunah Chineka living with her parents, Ropafadzo and Emmanuel Chineka in Harare, Zimbabwe.

Asia, Africa, Europe, North America ... four out of seven continents ... Mukai Mukundu Chapfumbu Mutubuki has seed everywhere!

What a phenomenal woman she was!!

Long live to Mukai Mukundu Chapfumbu Mutubuki's name and legacy!

Long live to all the great women in our families throughout all societies across the globe ... the unsung heroes ... the giants ... the pillars of strength!!

Long live to all the Matriarchs on this planet!!

I salute you ALL !!

May you continue to be the beacon of strength; the true North; the anchor and foundation your families need.

World, remember:

"The circumstances of your life will never describe the quality of your personality "~ Pastor Chris "So, step into your own POWER!!"~Bob Proctor

THE END

About The Author

Itai Vhudzijena is a Chartered Quantity Surveyor and an Intrapreneur.

A graduate of University of Kwazulu-Natal in Durban, South Africa, Itai Vhudzijena's professional career has seen her provide Cost Consultancy Services from South Africa, Zimbabwe, Botswana to The Middle East.

A loving mother of 2, Angela and Michael, Itai currently resides in Dubai